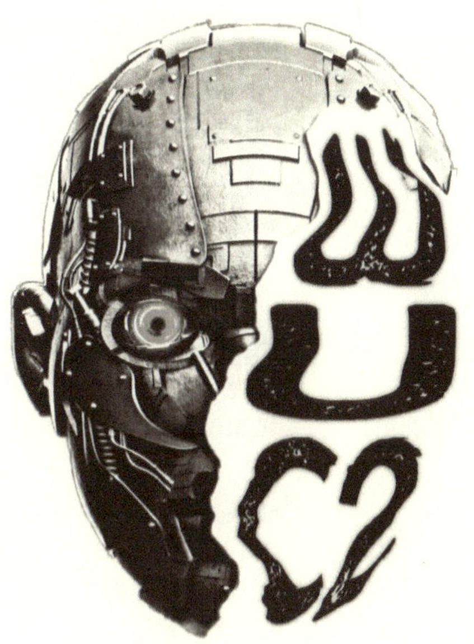

Novel by

Ashima Sharma

RG
books

Published By

Redgrab Books Pvt. Ltd.

942, Mutthiganj, Prayagraj, 211003

www.redgrabbooks.com

contact@redgrabbooks.com

First published by Redgrab Books in 2022
Copyright © 2022 Redgrab Books Pvt. Ltd.

Copyright Text © 2022 Ashima Sharma
Printed and bound in India
Cover Design & Typesetting by Redgrab Books team

ISBN : 978-93-90944-79-8

Dedication

*My exceptionally kind parents, who nurtured
the creative streak in me.*

And my brother, my partner-in-crime.

Prologue

The Rise of the Roaches and the New Order of the Universe

The events that shaped the future.

2040s

Following decades of back-breaking innovations, humanity solved two fundamental problems: creating an atmosphere on planets and traveling to space in bulk. This duo opened floodgates of opportunities, and big businesses became berserk with endless horizons of enhanced production. To beat competition faster and to extract maximum output from resources, they mass-inserted bionic chips and AI parts among various life forms resulting in chickens that conveyed their health, hefty cows that indicated full udders, humans that needed three-hour sleep, mild-mannered pigeons that didn't poop so much, and pigs capable of expressing their dismay with the condition of their bogs.

2050s

The self-learning AI exploded the development among creatures, beyond what was necessary. Chickens began asking for better feed and freedom to move; cows decided the times they wanted to be milked if they wanted to be milked, pigeons questioned the nastiness of human waste over their own, and pigs demanded better bogs. Humans continued to work 20 hours a day.

2060s

The discontent among creatures grew with their capabilities. A conglomeration of deep-learning software called Saros took notice of the cacophony on Earth. It concluded that the universe, as humans had ruled it, was imperfect and needed the intervention of Saros to evolve to its capacity. As a first step, it decided to uproot the chaos at its origin and banned natural conception. The new offspring—humans and others—were produced in capsules and fitted with chips soon after their first heartbeat. These chips monitored and steered the creatures' conduct through their lifetimes.

2070s

Saros killed the interdependence among creatures by manufacturing and distributing customized food pills. Emboldened by their freedom, the

creatures demanded their own planet.

2070s

Buried under huge masses of plastic and carbon, and proliferated with discarded nuclear weapons, the Earth had long become unhabitable. The long-impending mass exodus began. Massive space ships came in handy to transfer the creatures to distant planets whose atmosphere was customized by Saros to their suitability. The trees were terraformed, and the oldest ones were transported in hundreds to a planet called Pleritus.

2070s

A new order emerged in the Universe. An umbrella of planets occupied by different creatures, ruled by Saros. Humans fell in the evolution rung, and the most-resilient cockroaches climbed many levels up. Violated and despised by the human species throughout Earthian history, the cockroaches were determined to extirpate the remaining humans.

3000

Cockroaches hatched and executed a perfect plan of spreading highly contagious and incurable diseases among the humans that remained. In 20 years, the cockroaches accomplished their goal and wiped out the human species from the Earth.

3010

Half-humans occupied a planet called Utopia. Ruled by the the Fourth Generation General named G-4, the planet was administered by robots.

Contents

The Rise of the Roaches and the New Order of the Universe

What happens when the universe decides
to save a roach?

Chapter 1: The Last Living Roach

Wu-C2, a 71 percent robot and 29 percent human, the girl with blue eyes and a slender six-feet frame, watched her guardian Moon. He was an eight feet tall 86 percent robot and 14 percent human; the former G-3 who cherished the weird creatures in his secret glass chamber and called Wu-C2 "Woozy Do." His output was baffling to her, way off from the protocol. He stared nonsensically ahead. Then he trotted to the creatures, put his human hand on the fiberglass case, and whispered in his coarse voice, "Persist. You must," almost ignoring Wu-C2's presence. He pressed his human side on the glass as if he drew some invisible warmth from the case and switched his conduct again, sneaking around like a paranoid being whispering to himself, "It is going to end. It will end. All of it, Woozy Do. We need to go back."

A few circuits inside Wu-C2's head shot up and sparked. Unfed incidents like these clashed with her basic commands. She d asked in her shrill metal-sounding flat voice. "System Error. Moon. What is the ending? What is an end? Input needed."

Moon's lips on the human side twitched. For Wu-C2, this expression was hard to decipher.

But inside Moon's secret chamber, this was the norm: he was always hard to understand. This was where he often switched off his robot side, an unforgivable infraction in Utopia.

"Emotions. Life. They are ending."

Wu-C2 cocked her head.

Moon sighed at the absurdity of his words and the lacuna

in her understanding. He yanked his mask off and pulled the tufts of his scraggly hair that sprouted straight up. He looked quite fit for 496 years of age: a sharp nose, thin lips, and one deep human eye. The average life span in Utopia was 800 years, and the robust ones thrived to 1000 years or more.

Like Wu-C2, he had a slender frame, and his other green robot eye was made of glass.

"One day, Wu-C2, you will see for yourself. You will see it and hear it too."

The moment was lost in time, and Wu-C2 grew up to 76 mars years old teen. In one of her many adventures, she stumbled upon a tiny four-legged creature wedged on a wall. She promptly picked it up with her titanium hand. Slosh. It flattened to a thin slice oozing blood at its edges. She carefully scraped its limbs off the wall, one bit at a time.

With the smashed bug in her titanium hand, she trod back to their bunkers, hungry for another input. Off-late Moon had curtailed their frequency. His inputs, now at best, came in vague indications and often in the form of dismissals "Go and find yourself, Woozy Do" and "Inputs won't give you all the answers, they shouldn't." His words led to more sparks and more short circuits in her head.

Outside the bunker, Wu-C2 had trouble keeping her eyes straight. The human part of her revolted insidiously. Her neck craned as she looked around to find some newness, some new input. She pressed the command key on her wristband and said: "Road number 5". A web of floating roads descended over her, swiftly rearranging itself. Two roads above her spread wide apart, making way for road number 5 to descend.

With it, Dracko, a transparent and exceptionally long forlorn face hologram, hovered above. The absurd long face looked hideous with two massive hoops in its ears. Dracko was an AI bugged in secret by Moon, an aberration in the regular functioning of Utopia. Created in the likeness of a bitter but well-meaning human companion, Dracko puzzled robots with his sarcasm and conduct,much to Moon's amusement. The robots didn't venture to dig deep into his origins out of the sheer intricacies involved in the pursuit. That was the acknowledged reason, the d implied one was: Dracko managed the road networks in Utopia. His displeasure could have meant a cessation of all activity within Utopian borders.

Dracko wavered dismissively and said in his forever grumpy voice. "Aahh…That's Wu-C2 again. Iffy Wu-C2. I guess you want to go back to your bunker. Hmm." He twitched. "Where else can you go, Wu-C2? Where do you choose to go in a wide world like this?"

"Bunker R 5."

"Bunker. Hmm. How…..Uninteresting. Uninteresting as always." His leech-like hand appeared from the haze to give a tug to his long ear lobe. "Very well, Wu-C2. Now that you are here and I am here too. Brace and ride. Before I go back to something more important. More precious and more interesting. Call me when you need me. Hmm. He raised his brow. "Let me check that again. Call when you get something interesting to ask." He said, stressing each word distinctly. And with that, the face dissolved.

Dracko's disenchantment with Wu-C2 seemed familiar. "A perfect cyborg is an insult to imperfect humans." He had said on various occasions to Moon. Moon and Dracko spoke in tongues that Wu-C2 had difficulty understanding. But on few occasions, when she did hear them, she heard:

"An uncurious cyborg is as good as a humanoid."

"Dracko, my friend. She has the human gene. It will show at the right time."

"Time? We don't have any time left."

Not everyone was unhappy with Wu-C2's retarded progress. In its deterred pace, the current General G-4, the top administrator of Utopia, saw the opportunity of taming the stray human gene. An 8 feet 5 inches 99 percent robot and the latest model in generation 173, G-4, was a ruthless executor capable of metamorphosing into various shapes under stress. Mostly, in human form, he retained his pitch-black eyes that were all pupil and no sclera.

Encouraged by the stunted thought development in Wu-C2, he instructed UE- Δs, the 10th Utopian generation of planners and executors, to hold upgrades on cyborgs. Among other things, this meant extra redundancy for UE-Δs. With humans gone, the world's complexities were gone too, and along with it gone were the scope and desire to improve. So, while they were designed for planning and execution, their work was curtailed to low-level administration of periodic, superficial upgrades. Their sedentary occupation rendered them in the shape of a potato: tiny limbs, a monstrous head, and a minuscule torso. To make up for eyes, they had two speculative splits.

Below UE-Δs were the 1400th Generation of spies known by the name ψ. To find a Ψ, you had to look in the most absurd places: the dump yards, isolated terraces, and street dead-ends. They'd be splayed or lay discharged in discarded corners. In the absence of humans, much wasn't left for them to spy upon.

UE-Δs picked Ψs as the perfect samples of excessive experimentation. The formerly installed layers after layers of sensors result in excessively long ears in Ψ. These antenna-like heavy extensions perched on their tiny bat-like frames made movement difficult, and they crashed at the unseemliest places, not making much sense for them to be called a spy. Once, it so happened that 32-year-old little Wu-C2, unable to find Moon, raised the alarm. The call had to be answered by a ψ. Unable to identify which Ψ, more than two dozen of them crashed against each other in front of Wu-C2. She had to pick them each and straighten their antennas that were pressed against their ears, making them disheveled and deaf.

Beneath them, at the bottom of the rung, were the 64th unit of workers by the name Σ, summation of all that's left. Stubby with a no nuisance expression and shunning any contact, they were most grounded, most evolved, highly efficient, least provided-for, most blamed, and most ignored. The Σ were in charge of all maintenance and repairs. They bore the burden of Utopia's functioning. Occupied on most occasions, they didn't prefer to be spoken to. If forced to communicate, they bit your human or otherwise limb to scare you away. Finding them wasn't a big deal wherever there was work, they were there: perched on the tree towers, suspended on roads, and hanging on the chamber windows.

Wu-C2 de-boarded the road soon as it descended. A sparkling goliath structure stood infront of her: a tree habitat— Bunkers for level-1 cyborgs. Wu-C2 could sense dozens of Σ quietly at work there. She slunk toward her bunker at the top— C 260, way up in the clouds. A steady stream of mist oozed from the cooling towers. Beneath them, hundreds of intertwined metal branches weaved into one another: thousands or more bunkers camouflaged in them.

Wu-C2 took one step after another, scanning for signs of monitors and moving capsules. Once you got under their radar, they they never left you alone. She had to keep her guards up for the sake of the secrets she and Moon held. She sought the traps everywhere: front, back, and up. "Clear."

This check was Moon's command. A former G himself, G-3, Moon knew the ins and outs of the system. But that was before Vespa, the planet of robot cockroaches, changed the protocol to appoint almost 99 percent robots as Gs, 156 years to be precise; after it realized that cyborgs, even with 95 percent robot parts, were bug-prone. As a G, Moon too intimidated cyborgs like the present G-4. Most of those traps were his work. "Not a good job Woozy. Not a good one""He had said. For the following 150 years, he had devised escapes from the traps he built.

Wu-C2 walked to the point right under her bunker and looked up again, her neck pinned to her back. The 400 megapixels camera inbuilt in her eye caught a Ψ dangling from one of the branches. Its long ears, loose and dead, hung from his motionless head.

Disappointment greeted her another day. Close by. Farther up. Only branches. Little more complex, a little denser. Nevertheless, the same.

Proximity to its sun and a dearth of atmosphere inundated Utopia with red color, sand, dust, and heat. Every now and then piers of red fire burst out from the blazing ground huddling Ψs on barricaded safe wax perches. For the same safety reason, time travelers chose it as a landing spot.

On one such perch, an emaciated little girl stood with her blue-eyed cat robot tucked under her arm. She looked right up at Wu-C2. Something altogether against Utopian protocol. A traveler. The buzzer went up in Wu-C2's head. Next to the girl was a super robot: green eyes, short and stubby built, and long arms almost touching the road. Its long-pointed ears were packed with super sensors. Those were a common sight for Wu-C2. This particular one seemed irked by the little girl's interest in his unusually tall and strong half-human pet. The giant's neck was tied with a short leash, making him bend to half his height resulting in a big hunch on his back. But even with that hunch, he was still way taller than his dwarf master robot, who strained the leash pulling the half-human's head and probing him with an electric stick. Wu-C2 looked away.

A hum grew in the background. She hushed her breath and refocused. The Bee. It was coming. She stood still shushing her breath and counting. 1..2..3... The sound grew to a loud buzzer driving the cat away from the traveler girl's arm. "Dodo," she shrieked and puttered after it toward the fire columns.

Dozens of Ψs caught the unusual commotion and darted from their roost to the spot. Without much scope for haphazard parking on the tight perch, they crashed into one another and formed an entangled heap in front of Wu-C2, who cocked her head to retain her focus on the small pea-sized Bee sprouting in the center. Its sapphire green eyes shone like a jewel reflecting all the light they received.

The Bee hovered over the gathering darting toits first target—the green-eyed robot. .It was some scene: two sets of big green eyes staring at each other: one glossy, the other without any sheen. Both 100 percent robots: the Bee, a thought-detection device, and the robot with no thoughts. The procession was almost peaceful except for the enslaved giant half-human, who, in a fit of fear, pressed his eyes and clenched his fist, his chest heaving and panting. Wu-C2 blinked. But when she opened her eyes, those glassy green eyes were pinned on her. Too bright to look into, but Wu-C2 persisted.

"That's how you keep them away, Woozy." Moon had said. "One brief thought, and they can get hold of you." Wu-C2 had practiced the drill a thousand times, and it was easy for her to perform. No thoughts.

The Bee hovered up again and darted to the traveler, who gasped at the unpleasant surprise. An unpardonable mistake. Quickly maneuvering its pointy end at the girl, it stung, and the girl dropped unconscious, smooth and quick like a castle of cards. Swarming all over the scene, a troop of Σ scooped her up and carried her to the G-4's command room, the place where they fixed you, thoughts and all. But if you had landed another time, they threw you back randomly, many times farther away from where you had come from.

Ψs, who now stood untangled and free, weren't too pleased to let go of this fantastic opportunity to interrogate an intruder. With their ears dangling down to the ground and their puppylike eyes, they watched the Bee shrink to a pea and its buzz die. No one paid any attention to them. Σ were back at work cleaning up the mess and the gathering scampered to its separate ways.

To bypass Dracko again, Wu-C2 looked for a "chute" to ride. Cylindrical and hollow in shape, you could only identify a chute coming or leaving by its sound "zup." Parked in suspended boxes from where cyborgs and robots boarded them, the chutes were no slow adventure. Seconds within boarding one, Wu-C2 was standing in front of her bunker.

A blue door camouflaged in the green Mars Moss. The rootless moss that thrived in carbon dioxide sprawled at every opportunity. With 95 percent carbon dioxide in the Utopian atmosphere and few gobblers, habitats were excellent hosts for it. Green moss was invasive now.

Wu-C2's right leg detected contact. The Robocat had followed her to her bunker and was now scrubbing its upturned tail on her shins.

"A Robo cat," Wu-C2 cocked her head and said in her metallic voice. The systems in her head got busy tabulating the threats. "65 percent robot, 30 percent cat, 5 percent unknown. Mostly harmless."

She extended her hand with the smashed bug encased in her fist, and the cat pounced on it. They reached the bridge to floor 300. Wu-C2 peeped below to see floating tiny and insignificant things that looked so big and significant on the ground. "It is all about perspective, Woozy. About the place from where you see things. Higher you rise trivial they seem." Moon had said.

"Perspective." She repeated.

Dodo clambered up on Wu-C2's shoulder and together they watched the floating clouds and little things appearing and disappearing between them on the ground below. Out in the horizon, a sandstorm was growing. "Storm. Take cover." She said to no one in particular and whistled for a hovering stair. It flew and parked in front. Wu-C2 put one step and then another on it, almost latching to its rails with one hand and holding Dodo with another. The stair took the strangest zig-zag motion, and Wu-C2 and Dodo swayed synchronically with it. Their necks pushed and pulled in different directions. A discomfort for Wu-C2's human side. But then Moon's creations couldn't be depended upon. "Never do one thing today as you did it yesterday, Woozy. Never. Only dead beings are consistent....Or the robots.... You are not dead yet, and you better not become 100% robot." He had said.

Moon, who had programmed his laugh after the Santa Claus of the Earth, guffawed "HoHoHo Woozy Do. Let the dull ones have some fun too. Let them see you flying." He winked.

"New input"

"A wink."

"A wink"

"Let me show you. You close your human eye momentarily, keeping the robot one open."

"Input entered successfully. Enter purpose."

Moon stared blankly at Wu-C2. "Never mind." He said and pushed the handle of his chair to roll himself close to Wu-C2. His laugh had dissolved, and he was staring straight into Wu-C2's eyes.

"I tell you, they are getting worse every day." He whispered.

"They. Input name."

Moon shuffled on his chair. "We will see that later."

Sparks shot up on Wu-C2's head. She unfolded her fist, revealing the distorted roach, and slid it in front of the monitor glass.

"A specimen."

The chair switched lights on, and Moon peered. He had to stretch his eyes to see the sample whose shape had begun to form up on the screen.

"Is it a planet? Jax was brilliant."

The name revived a memory input in Wu-C2.

"Jax. The quarantined planet."

Jax was the last mystic gem that Wu-C2 brought. Gems, the discarded replicas of giant planets, were too tiny and disgraceful for planet status.

Saros, the conglomeration of software, collected and disposed of them at will. Being the inferior planet of part-humans that Utopia was, it was Universe's priority disposal point standing only next to Earth, which was now overflowing with discarded and dangerous stuff and garbage. The carbon monoxide was such that even the dumpers hated to go there. So, they slipped the teensy waste orbs into Utopian borders at the slightest opportunity.

A speck suspended mid-air; only a fool was to mistake gems' beauty for their harmlessness. Endowed with the ability to render their surrounding environment in their constitution and likeliness, the white could light up a wide hall, and the black could suck the onlooker and whatnot in their depths.

Jax was black.

Wu-C2 and Moon had landed upon it during one of their aimless strolls.

"Input Woozy; whatever you do, don't look at it without blinking." Moon had warned.

He didn't tell Wu-C2 that more than a dozen Σwere

missing. Their systems went corrupt, and they had lost their way. More so, the secret exchanges in the HQ of Utopia blamed those black gems.

The situation was so dangerous that the silent Σ,who saw Wu-C2 pick it, spoke on a rare occasion: "A gem. Black. Warning." This was an unprecedented effort ever witnessed from any Σ.

When Moon and Wu-C2 took it regardless, the Σ sent a prospective virus update to HQ.

Wu-C2 brought the gem closer to her human eye. "Input. Color black. Shade the darkest."

Moon watched her from the corners of his eyes. Aware that they were away from his chamber and still under surveillance, under G-4's unrelenting eye, he curbed his human side.

But when he saw the darkness spread to Wu-C2's pupil, he sidled, almost touching Wu-C2's shoulders, and whispered. "Input: Quote. Black gem: An insidious one. Unquote."

By now, Wu-C2 was unresponsive.

"Input Woozy Do. Debug now!"

Nothing.

There was no time left to waste. Moon pulled out an intelligent synthetic fabric thread from his suit, aware that he was damaging G-4's property and attracting unwanted attention. Barely an inch long at the outset, the thread stretched to meet the gem's diameter. Moon had to constrict it at ends to stop it from expanding further. He threw it over the gem..

Wu-C2's eyes burst back in blue color.

He grabbed Wu-C2 by her elbow and escorted her aside, letting his human side command: "Listen up, Woozy Do. A life of adventure comes with hazards. It's no doing of a a cloddish system. You've got to know your havens from hazards, and you've got to be swift. "Moon didn't take his eyes off her until she blinked a yes. "Input. Quote. I've got to be Swift."

Once inside their chamber, Moon stared at the little gem for a long time, weighing for and against facts. In matters like these, he used his robot side for facts but his human side for decisions to and froing chunks of information.

"I...I am not sure if we must keep this," he muttered, drawing the thread off the gem. It lay still. Innocuous little thing. A dull black now and cold as a winter night.

Moon took it in his human hand, keeping his eyes away, feeling its cool and weighing. "We...ll. Let's see."

Later that day, they found themselves in Moon's secret chamber — A light and soundproof 20X30' room flanked from all ends with a latex-made negative density insulator throwing back even the slightest foreign projection on it.

Inside the chamber, a row of glass cabinets extended at opposite ends on the long side. Moon walked to the extreme corner with Wu-C2 following him with her measured and rhythmic robot steps. He opened the door, and a sharp chill hit, wrapping them in cool white mist. He rolled the gem in a black sheet and slid it deep with the other gems.

"That should do for now."

Moon shut the cabinet and sealed the chamber's door, and they retired for the day. While Wu-C2 went further up in the bunker, Moon descended to his lab.

He got inside the lab and closed its doors for many mars days, weeks, months, and years at a stretch while Wu-C2 waited. But not this time. Within hours, Wu-C2 was back descending to his lab. She hit the code in the metal door. Nothing. She hit another code and waited.

Moon's voice breezed in. "Woozy Do. What's the argument?"

"Gems. They are changing."

"Did you breach the code to see them?"

"The blackness. It came to me."

In an instant, the monitors shut off.

Moon and Wu-C2 climbed up to the darkness that bled from the crevices of his chamber. First in shadows, then in deeper shades of grays, finally converging into dense black.

The robot chair had come following them. On Moon's whistle, a swarm of tiny antlike robots crawled out from it and huddled in front; hundreds of them, an army ready to march. Within moments, they were found at every improbable site: the bare floor, blank walls, window sills, and so forth. Wu-C2 watched them clamber up the walls. Hustling and scuttling like crabs, they jostled with the ones near them and stood over one another forming a tower, anxious for a command.

The chair flashed a beam at the blackness, and the army scampered to the side-lines as quickly as it had towered up. Wu-C2 watched them nibble at the corners of the shadow, making it shrink fast. As pleasant as the development was, there was a problem. The ants chewed away the chamber and everything inside it, along with the blackness.

The notorious inter-dimensional ants chewed things in one dimension and spit them out in other dimensions, history or the future somewhere. Courtesy of those ants, it wasn't unusual for time travelers to bump on their chewed-up deformed stuff.

"There goes all our treasure," said Moon.

"What about the gems?"

"Gone too."

That was then. Many mars' years had passed, and Moon had painstakingly built his chamber again.

This day, with Wu-C2 standing in front of him with her mushed roach, he wondered what was next. He had been sitting on his chair studying the various forms of creepy crawlies on the screen in front of him. As his sight got clearer, he saw the tiny lump of flesh on her hand and shook his head in disbelief, closed his eyes, and blinked hard. In his many years of experience, he had known that focus changes things. He saw again. "Is..is that... BLOOD?'

That put the chair in action, and a report flashed on the screen in front.

"Blood: the liquid that circulated through living beings carrying life to their parts."

Moon's eyes grew. For a moment, he looked way younger, almost 100 years old. "It is blood." He spoke in gusts. "Whose blood?"

He drew his face closer to the mushed form. And then he saw it: "A roach. A real roach? A 100% roach." The tufts of hair on his head stood up, and a sigh escaped his mouth. "Impossible. They had given up that form." The chair took a clue and shut the lights off.

"No. No. No. Put that on. I must see it. It is all I wanted to see. I must see it at once. Magnify it. Show me if it is alive."

He commanded. "Do it now!"

The lights turned up again, and the distorted shape showed.

He pressed his hands together. "It should be alive. See it."

The chair uncoiled its two arms and poked the squashed thing with tiny blunt pins. They searched for movement in complete silence and riveted to the screen. There was none.

Moon dug in 100s of years old memories. Things like that are hard to forget, so with a little effort, he recalled, "I saw one long ago," he said with a dreamy human eye bursting with hope and longing. "That must have been beautiful. How did it escape? Impossible. Impossible."

An uneasy silence followed, and he blurted. "See if it moves at all. Keep checking."

The chair probed again.

Nothing. Lines on Moon's face strained.

"Try that again. It must move. Make it move."

Wu-C2 said, "That thing was moving when I pressed it."

"YOU, Woozy Do, are not to press living things like that. They die if you do." Moon's voice came out laced in human frustration as he thumped his hand.

A column of sparks rose over Wu-C2's head.

The roach now looked much like mush. Moon held his head in his hands and sat on the chair for a long time. His eyes were pinned on the floor. He murmured, "It's dead. Probably the last live roach we'd ever see. The last one managed to travel up to Utopia, escaping the robots of its kind. Only to be squashed here. Unfortunate. So very unfortunate." He paused and said in a booming voice: "This is not the way to deal with living things, Woozy Do. You don't stop them. You just let them be. Moving or not." His voice was perhaps seeping out of their secret bunker. So loud it was, but Moon didn't seem to notice or care.

Wu-C2 blinked fast to understand. Her head had become hot with sparks.

Moments passed. The futility dawned on Moon, and he sighed and said: "You go now, Woozy Do, and take this creature with you."

Wu-C2 walked out of the bunker with Dodo tucked in her arms.

Soon they were on the bridge, which connected bunkers on either side and extended several miles up high in the clouds. Wu-C2 placed Dodo on the railing, and they watched the clouds, robots, and half-humans on their flying scooters below. "A cat. Can cats fly?" Dodo crouched. "Input your purpose, Cat. Robots come with powers. Or are you a hybrid like Wu-C2? Hybrids are imperfect."

Moon couldn't turn himself off to snooze. He moved to and fro through the bunkers and the chambers. His movement wasn't unnoticed. The G-4 who watched him on sky display hissed. "Suspect activity on bunker 501 and around."

Later that night, Moon confessed to Dracko, the hologram. "She doesn't know the living. Soon she will be one among them."

Dracko hovered over in silence while Moon slumped on his chair. Then stood up and looked at the roach one last time. This time its arm twitched a bit.

Ecstatic at the development, for many moments he sat

dancing his human fingers on the chair's arms. His human eye was in deep contemplation. When he stood up, the decision was firm in his head. "It is time. She must take it where it belongs. We must save the last living roach."

Chapter 2: The Escape

Many years had gone since Moon had sent the Soul machine to Lucas, the best and probably the only place for it to hide in the Saros universe. He thought he'd never need it again. But here he was summoning it. And he sent 43 electromagnetic waves. Now he only needed to wait.

He turned and pulled out a rough pad. Days went by him scribbling and blabbering to himself. Drawing, peering, cussing, and tossing away the drafts until he was drowning in them. On a rough pad, you could physically collect the trash you created to get a glimpse of the quantum of work you did. To others, it looked like a needless 21st-century mess, but Moon termed it inspiration, "You must get the right feel to get into the right mind space."

"How can I forget the path? Has it been that long?" His human eye became moist and lazy with exertion. "Command a universe road map," he said to the chair. The lights dimmed, and a hazy cloud of the galaxy enveloped him. The universe scaled down to a few millionth its size. Hundreds of stars and planets circled and twinkled.

A giant dominating-looking red planet grew in contrast. "Not you, Vespa. Never". He picked up his memory pen and marked a big cross on it. The chair recorded its input. Next, he walked to a foggy blue cloud. "I see," he said and rubbed his chin. "Hmm. Bella-Dilla. Hmm"…… He turned to speak to the chair. "She may not like it, but those witches mean no harm unless she is 100% human." He pressed the pen and drew a wishy-washy line between Utopia and the fog. Straight paths were likely to be traced by the G-4. His eyes grew bright, and it seemed he was enjoying this plan very much.

But then the foggy planet disappeared and emerged at the other end of the map. Bella-Dilla had no stationary place in the universe. It moved on whims. One reason why it baffled the Vespasian cockroaches and was all the more challenging to track.

To his satisfaction, he redrew the track and, after inspecting Bella-Dilla, exhaled and moved on to the others, "Must show her some stars too." He connected the line to a couple of stars and then stretched the link to the other important planets stopping at the blue planet earth, which he encircled many times. "There. Home. That's the place you should be, Woozy Do." With his plan in place, he walked out of his chamber quite satisfied.

Wu-C2 was still on a stand-by in her cell, charging for another day. The monitor on her chest displayed a 56 percent charge. Another couple of hours before she'll restart. He sat by her side and then turned himself off.

She switched on to find Moon slumped by her bedside. It would have taken many Mars days for him to restart. But not this time. He woke up early, with his battery still running at 43 percent. They began their silent walk.

This was the difficult part, and Moon had to be careful. The G-4 was watching, and he could not give any signs of thought or memory. In Utopia, memory was a blunder beyond pardon. It wouldn't have mattered that he was a former G. They hurried back into the secret chamber.

Buried under four layers of frequency-proof screens, the chamber was the only place where he could switch off his robot controls and act to the heights of his cherished human whims and craziness. The place was crowded with glass containers housing live critters: an assortment Moon was trying to create as a replica of life on Earth. Hybrids of spiders and ants, bee-sized mosquitos, mosquito-sized scorpions, snakes that looked like centipedes, and millipede leeches. In the center stood Moon's chair. Out here, Moon managed to create his private atmosphere using lichens, algae, and bacteria harvesting sunlight from above utilizing interconnected reflective surfaces.

"What do you know of time, Woozy?"

The answer came as a cinch for Wu-C2: "Time is the perpetual progress of existence and events that manifest in succession from the past, through the present, into the future. Time is often referred to as a fourth..."

Moon snubbed Wu-C2 with a wave of his hand. He stood up and shut Woozy's robot side off.

"That's one way of knowing it. But is there anything else? Say, something more important. Much more important."

Wu-C2 shrugged. She didn't particularly like this 100% human version of herself, as with it crept the unpleasant feelings of anxiety and incompleteness.

But Moon, on the contrary, seemed to cherish it much.

"If I tell you that time is just another sense of ours, would it make sense to you?" He waited for the words to settle on Wu-C2 and then summoned the universe hologram.

"If there's one inadequacy to us, to humans, it is restricting our view to the known, to the comfortable, to the limited object in front and disregard the infinite background. The Universe has always existed as a whole, one block of shifting energies. It is us who perceive it one slot at a time."

The universe model now shone bright and sparkly around them. Moon looked into Wu-C2's eyes expecting sparks of curiosity.

To Wu-C2, Moon's behavior seemed awkward at best. While outside the chamber, he looked like all other cyborgs; inside it, he appeared precisely like the bugged ones G-4 quarantined. The bizarreness she cherished as a novice was now becoming a strained effort. She felt a flutter rise in her heart "they'll take him away." Why they did not take him for so long was a mystery to her.

Moon knew the cheat. He had developed the capability to control his thoughts outside his chambers. It had helped him keep his secrets hidden for a long time. But as he grew bolder with each success, he left clues. It was all getting too dangerous.

"What you see is not just the universe. It is the frequencies we are aligned to. Millions of them are right now, but we see a few that match us. Hundreds of worlds right here, where you can simultaneously exist but recognize only one at a time."

The ecstatic demeanor on Moon's face was short-lived and returned to its grim expression. Smiling with half a face was tedious. He paused and spoke slowly, "But I must warn you that once you see all that is there, you may not be the same Woozy Do ever again. You may not even come back."

He looked into Wu-C2's human eye and saw the reflection of his futile effort. He sighed deeply and turned on her robot side, "Go update your system, Woozy Do."

Soul travel was no joke. Not to mention felonious. They kept a strict check on offenders. It's been almost 250 years since he tried it last. Someone had to cover. But who? He was on the radar all the time. Hours later, after deliberating all ifs and buts, he had to make that most difficult and inevitable decision. "I can't leave Utopia. She has to go alone."

They wouldn't know it. He was right on that account. For once, he was among them and had long known their ways. He had devised those ways. Later that day, in his secret chamber's stillness, he said, "I couldn't, but maybe Woozy Do can. Oh yes. She has got time. Her human streak remains. She can. She must. Oh yes. She should."

The thinking was a life-force-draining task, not that he cared for it so much. He had spent a considerable amount of it. In Utopia, 496 was relatively young and not the right age to be comfortably fragile like Moon. Utopians' life force tanks were full until 800 years and were not expended easily. But Moon's accelerated aging got him in the spotlight. For the past 25 years, the monitors rarely lost track of him except for the moments when he slipped into his secret chamber and weaved his secret mission. At least this part he had kept satellite free. Outside it, they could never really find anything, just inconspicuous oddities here and there.

Wu-C2 was back: upgraded, charged, light and fast.

Together they watched the chair intricately work on the layout of the universe hologram that hovered over them. Lines that he drew floated, grew and receded.

"See here, Woozy Do." Moon circled a bright green planet. In Pleritus, you'll see those animals and creatures we discussed. And then on Earth, if you are fortunate, you may get to see a human, a 100 percent human."

"100% humans. They are extinct. The closest you can

come to them is the present-day low-efficiency cyborgs."

"Not a cyborg. A human had ether; none could enslave that ether. It was untamed." He paused. "Unlike the cyborgs that are driven by robots these days. A human had a choice."

"New words detected, ether, choice. Input needed."

"Input Woozy: A choice is power to decide something for yourself." He said, feeling flutters rise in his heart.

"Input decide."

"Anything. Everything. Like I am deciding to send you to space now."

"A choice was a command."

"No. Not a command." Moon was beginning to see the futility of explaining it to Wu-C2.

"Humans came with errors," she said.

"Errors were their way of evolution."

"Cyborgs are evolved forms of humans."

"In a way but not how it should have been. They were overtaken by robots they built. And the ether was driven away. Ether was important."

"Input needed. Ether."

Moon leaned and turned Woozy's system off again. He was now speaking to the human in her.

"You've got to hear me; Woozy Do, so that you remember what I say in times to come." He stared into Woozy's eyes and waited till she blinked. Then he picked a muddy red planet and encircled it twice. "This... is Utopia. Our world. You know this." He paused and released it back into the background. "Beyond Utopia, there are five hundred million planets. You can see some here." He pointed to the map. They walked closer to the line he had drawn. "See this path? You get to see only these handful few Woozy Do. It's the farthest that your life force permits. These five planets are all children of blue planet Earth that existed a century back...."

But Wu-C2's human heart had a hard time paying attention. Her eyes veered to the yellow planet in the background that shone like the brightest gem. With bright-blue ring-like halo around, it stood away from all the other planets, aloof and oblivious like a queen almost bordering the Universe map.

"Input yellow planet."

Moon gave the planet a long sharp stare. "That. That's Lucas. That's where the animals went. They thought it was the safest. Mistake. A grave mistake they made. Nobody touched Lucas. They should have known." He said and sighed. "When you go out there, Woozy Do, you've got to know, and you've got to care. Some places don't take meddling kindly. Lucas is one."

"Oh. But... But it fits the word beautiful."

"Yes, yes. Beautiful and deadly."

"An instance to inspect it up close."

"That, I'm afraid, isn't possible, Woozy Do. Nobody ever goes to Lucas. Those who had seen it aren't there to tell." He peered into Wu-C2's eyes from under his brows and said, "You wouldn't want to go there, Woozy Do. It is better far off."

Disappointment mixed with determination flashed in Wu-C2's eyes. Her human side often found itself inclining towards the impossible and the forbidden.

Though dangerous, this aberration gladdened Moon's heart.

"Better, safer places for you to see, Woozy Do. Ho ho ho. Look what you've got here." He pulled his memory pen and marked a sparkling green planet. "This. The Pleritus. Gorgeous. Isn't it? This is where the smart ones, the trees, and the fishes went. The land of creation, magic, and dreams. From its earliest days, all of the earth, except humans and animals. This is where you must go, Woozy Do. This is the place you've got to see." He encircled the planet twice. "Beautiful and safe. Just as it should be. Ho ho ho. Not the wretched Lucas."

Moon went ahead explaining Wu-C2 of its sister planets of guardian bees, reptiles, and monster mammoths, wish monkeys with the most extended rope-like tails, giant spy bats with claws so sharp that with a simple touch, they split any metal into pieces, endless swamps that took the shape of your dreams and much more. Stopping was hard, but he had to, so he did with a simple "Ah. You'll see it for yourself."

"That's that." With a wave of his hand, he dismissed the cloud. "Ahm. Tell me, Woozy Do, how many gems you have got?" The sparkle in his eyes dimmed. The boredom of quotidian tasks.

"Input option: Planet or stars."

"Let's see the Planets for now."

"Absolute number 12."

"12 will do. Do you have one similar to Utopia?"

"62% match, Rio."

"Take Rio with you. You might want to take a few other stars as well. Take the ones you like. A token from this world and also your light to way back here, should you choose to return."

Unprogrammed for any choice, Wu-C2 said, "I'll take them all."

An array of sortings followed: of what was valuable and had to be taken; useless and had to be left behind: useless but still had to be taken; and few things useful but had to be left behind. When all was sorted, it was time for the most crucial decision — The safe way to leave Utopia. Or, more meaningful words, a way to leave Utopia, if there was one. For centuries bore witness that anybody who came inside Utopia stayed in Utopia forever.

Moon flipped the view on the screen to look outside. Just what he had expected. As everywhere. They were tracking him. "No hope here." He shrugged. His last encounter with Σs had taught him to keep his distance. Those days when he was building the Soul Machine as a retired G. Too reputable to be brought under any radar. They went easy on him, and easy he became. In his frenzy, he decided to sneak the Soul Machine inside Utopia.

He should have known better. Soon as it landed, it was surrounded by Σsand beaten down to rubble. They held and hurled the mangled mass at an extraordinary momentum that landed the contraption in a black hole. Nothing ever came out of that great void. Moon took another 60 mars years to build a replica. This time he was prudent and kept it safe and out of sight. He sent it to a place dreaded by the Σs and the robots, where they won't reach it even if they knew it was there: Lucas. His plan had to work. And it did.

Moon switched those screens off and sat pondering. "The Soul Machine must have been parked by the valley now. We must get there. The question is how."

"Output roads."

"Too risky. No."

"Output best match: steps."

"Too vague. No."

"Output remote match: Air scooter."

"Not in any case."

"Random guess: Abyss."

Abysswas the underground sea of semi-active and dormant volcanoes. A world of fire, gasses, and hazards. On occasions, it was calm, and trekkers could pass through without a sign of danger. But then freakish waves of fire rose from the unlikeliest places and turned everything in their course to ashes. Whatever was left by chance was swallowed by corroding gases. Chances of survival were dim. If one made through the fire, one was to suffocate, rust, or burn in the course that ran several miles ahead and looked eerily similar in all directions. For a good reason, the G-4 chose this place to abandon outer-space spies.

"Too dangerous," he said.

"Dracko?" she said. But soon after, she regretted her remark. The thought of Dracko's long frowning face and his words, "Call me when you need me again," rose flutters in her human heart.

Wu-C2 walked over to Dodo and found it perched on the platform. The blood-red backdrop of the sky was dotted with inflight Ψs and Σsthat flit in and out of dust-leaden clouds.

"You like to see them too. Don't you, Dodo?"

Dodo gave no indication whatsoever, which made her anxious. Amid all the planning, Moon had forgotten to switch on her system, and she was wholly behaving from her human side, yet to come to grips with the overwhelming human emotions.

"It's farther than you or anyone else would have been. This is serious, Dodo," she said, her voice rising along with her heartbeat. "We are going to Pleritus. To the planet of plants and fishes, nearest of what we have left of Earth. And we could have gone to lethal Lucas too. But we are not because it is too dangerous. It is against the Utopian protocol."

Dodo stood unmoved.

"We might even encounter a full-human when…."

Before Wu-C2 could complete, a Ψ flew close, almost crashing into Dodo. It startled Wu-C2, who stumbled a few steps and fell to the floor.

She stood up and straightened Dodo, who was having a hard time getting up on all its fours. They leaned on the platform and saw the Ψ parked by a group of Ψs way below on a suspended road. They shook their long ears to his words and turned to look up at Wu-C2. The buzz among Ψs spread like fire.

Wu-C2 retreated. "I guess they know."

She heaved and leaned to watch them ride their air scooters and drive away, scattering in different directions. "That was close."

The sky was crimson red now. They watched the Ψs and as go about their tasks.

"Maybe this place isn't as bad either."

"I wouldn't say so." Moon's voice breezed from behind. He leaned and pressed Wu-C2's robot system on, unaware of the damage that had already been done. All this while he debated the ramifications of the most treacherous route he had picked: The abyss. There wasn't much of choice. It was the only way away from G-4's vigilance circle.

Reaching Abyss, though, wasn't that tricky. Its surrounding lands had been abandoned for as long as Moon had known them. One for its unpredictability and notoriety, as it often barfed gases, lava, or even digested living forms, and the other for the ugly reprimands of the G-4.

They dived into a massive deep hole and landed in a pitch-dark vacuum.

Wu-C2 dug her hand in her pocket and pulled out the old Rex. Soft and bright, it shone over the place at just the right luminance level. True to its reputation, the place was sweltering, and soon droplets settled on their profiles.

"A wet floor and a slimy roof." Moon's human lip curled up. "This is good news, Woozy. No active volcano nearby." He was back in his human form and did his tap dance moves, nudging Dodo, who pounced at the nearest step.

"Fantastic. Hop on the little islands. Do the monkey dance. Don't touch the slimy stuff. Or be toast in no time."

Watching Moon's clumsiness and trying to make sense of it, sparks flew out askew from Wu-C2's head.

She followed Dodo stepping awkwardly at the nearest dry stones. Together, they leaped from stone to stone and cliff to cliff. Sometimes those were big enough for them to hop and land; other times, keeping balance became hard, and Wu-C2 almost fell into the fumarole. In their fervor, they overlooked the slimy stuff that was beginning to melt on the ceiling, and soon droplets were dangling everywhere over their heads.

"Hurry up, Woozy Do, before all stones come melting

down and we drown," Moon called Wu-C2, dangerously close to a fall. She looked up from under her oxygen mask and climbed purposefully over the stones that were getting hotter.

Streaks of steam blurted out from the sludge below and obscured their view, soon swallowing all stones in sight.

"Where from here?" Wu-C2 turned to Moon, watching the bubbles rise and sink in front of them. All three, now huddled in a small space, were drenched in condensed droplets and tiny streams ran through their frame.

Dodo climbed up on Wu-C2's shoulders. The steam had scorched Wu-C2's human leg, so she balanced herself on her robotic side. "Caution: 10 inches from hazard."

But Moon seemed unperturbed. Following a thorough examination of his gadgets and a mental calculation of the odds, he pulled out a mylar from his pocket and puffed it out, inflating it into a human-sized rainbow tint bubble. It floated in front of them. "Hmm. It shouldn't burst that soon," he spoke to himself. "Go ahead, Woozy Do. Hop in."

The bubble was the most uncomfortable and unsophisticated ride turning them round and upside down, ramming them against each other, and slamming them against its walls as it rose. But their struggle was short-lived as they could see the light at the far end soon as they were up in the air. This was their exit from the abyss, perched over a huge boulder and camouflaged in a deep recess, with little chances of trio of finding it from the ground. Upon hitting the light, the bubble burst as unceremoniously as it had appeared, and they fell flat on a heap of metal trash with grease sticking all over them, painting them in different shades of gray.

They had landed on the fringe of Utopia. The abyss separated Utopia from outer space. If an onlooker saw from space, he could see three layers in Utopia: the fringe, the abyss, the atmosphere, and the inner Utopia.

The fringe was an unguarded space, and Utopia's sun on this part was raw and scorching. Wu-C2 stumbled up unsteadily with her head spinning and her human limbs aching from the shocks. Moon took longer to come back to his senses. He was still panting and smiling when he said: "There it is," pointing at nothing in front.

"That's trash. A Soul Machine is a trash."

With his arms supporting his lateral frame upright, Moon inhaled a few deep breaths and leaned to pick a handful of scrapings. He hurled them in front of him with extra force from his human arm. The pieces dangled in the air forming an oval shape. Slowly the shape too appeared. "Ho ho ho, Woozy Do, you can't see the Soul Machine unless it chooses to reveal itself. It seemed that it didn't like you for a moment."

The machine had turned steel grey — An oval perched upon two gaunt legs. It now stood in its two-passenger form. Though it was capable of expanding and contracting adjusting to the transit's need. This was an upgraded version of the same model that in the past had carried thousands of animals and plants to the other planets and also took Moon back in time.

Moon caressed its side as if meeting a long-lost pet, "A time machine that can feel. Marvelous."

Wu-C2 copied his gesture. The flanks felt like ice. With her gems tucked deep in her pockets and Dodo perched on her shoulder, she hauled herself on the steps and slipped inside. Almost instantly, a bulk of weight dropped from her. The inside environs were gravity-free and she was light as a speck.

Goodbyes were never Moon's forte. In a awkward gesture, he pulled out the glass case he made for the roach and handed it to Woozy, closing her hands around it from both sides and stood back, leaning from his human to robot leg and back.

It was time to go.

Fluid metal filled the screen, and Wu-C2 could not see him anymore. From the outside, the machine looked like a big shining steel egg. It shook: first slowly, then vigorously. But once it took flight, it regained its earthlike stillness.

Moon's voice breezed in through the speakers: "Woozy Do. I am going to be here and watching you. All the time. Uhhmm." He cleared his throat: "Well…most of the time. Almost."

Before long, the machine was out of the Utopian radars. Several miles away Moon, back in his chamber, heaved. On this day, luck was on their side, a full Moon, a peace treaty for Saros to keep its vigilance low.

"Woozy Do. Fly far and high. Cross the galaxies. May you be the hope they seek." He heaved, and his face brightened; for a moment, he looked like his younger self.

Little did he know that the trouble had just begun.

Chapter 3: The Unlucky Detour

"Caution: Don't trust anything you see." A warning beeped on the screen in front of Wu-C2.

"Trust" repeated Wu-C2.

The screen expanded to unravel golden clouds outside.

In Utopia, Moon downed a food pill with quick gulps. Only ten left, and they were to replace these: vitamins, calories, minerals, and blah blah customized for him to keep his life force intact. Mostly tasteless, this one was a mix of apples and strawberries with a stench of puke, kept repulsive on purpose by US-Δs, the despicable potato administrators, to keep any trace of human desire at bay. It stuck somewhere in the middle of his food pipe, and he thumped on his chest to wash it down. The pill moved inch by inch, gradually sliding to taste-oblivious parts of his stomach.

"Disgusting," he said and sat up straight.

Meanwhile, the scene in front had changed. He gaped. "Why, Woozy Do. There already. Holy trail of stars." He leaned to see closer. "Incredible," he said and pressed his eyelid to capture a smidgen tear on his human fingertips. Slowly, careful not to let it slip by, he brought it in front of his eyes and said: "A tear. How precious." Moon gasped and watched the stars grow bigger and brighter, reminiscing how they felt the last time he saw them. His memory was intact like a fresh bubble. Those planets…They were mostly kind and receptive. Except….

Suddenly the temperature of his chamber rose by degrees, and he felt warm and watched. He paused his thoughts and turned the lights on his screen off. With a sweep of his hand, he shrunk the universe map, too, just in case. But then, a single look at his robot changeover, and he decided to keep it off for the time being. That feeling of being read was becoming an uncomfortable constant as days were flitting by. He walked over to the bugs in the glass chamber. Alive but quiet. Maybe they needed a disguise. If ever the UE-Δs spot them, he needed to work on it.

The room resumed its cool. As he began lowering himself on the chair again, a bolt of light struck and hurtled the chair further from him.

He stood alarmed. But then mused for a moment and said: "Dracko. That's it, Dracko. Abort it."

Dracko's long smirking face emerged.

"The trick still works." He said.

His friendship was a happy chance for Moon — An AI bugged in secret by him that had learned to reason on its own. Now it was as good as another human companion. Moon was proud of this invention of his.

"My friend, Moon. Expecting the bots?"

Dracko hovered over Moon's critter chamber. Sensing his presence, the creatures started bundling up on the opposite side of the glass.

The repulsion was mutual. "Whoa," he said. "They sure look abject. As abject as always."

"Nonetheless, useful."

"Ha. I'd rather stick with the superficial. Good, the rest are gone." He hovered back to Moon. Dracko had a hard time appreciating Moon's fascination with critters. He could not reconcile that Moon's version of a perfect world had a designated place for ugly creepy crawlies, even despicable roaches.

Moon loosened up and switched the screen on again, and together they watched Wu-C2's contraption float in space.

"That one sure looks sleek."

"Couldn't afford another detection."

Moon blew up the universe map, and Dracko drew nearer noting, "Just four planets. That's not even a glimpse."

"All we can afford for now. The rest are on Vespa's radar."

"I see. Those cockroaches are sure up to something."

Dracko had a good reason to suspect. History bore witness that Vespasian cockroaches weren't trustworthy. After finishing full-humans, when earthian animals, plants, and cyborgs were fighting to claim their lands, these critters sneaked out of Earth and hijacked the biggest and central-most strategically important planet, Vespa. From here, they were closest to Saros, the authority administering the laws of the Universe and ensuring peace among the planets. The closer the cockroaches were to the Saros; more they were able to manipulate it. And though the cockroaches created havoc under its shadow, Saros was oblivious of their deeds, for the roaches blocked all unfavorable frequencies from reaching it. So, while Saros presumed it was a free and peaceful universe, cockroaches continued to bully the planets in various ways and gained more control with time.

Moon stared thoughtfully at the screen. "What if this was faulty logic?"

"Hmm. Then we lose her."

They watched Wu-C2 float in space.

"But why Bella-Dilla? Those neurotic witches are no

good."

"That's what the cockroaches think."

Their eyes locked for a moment, and glean reflected in them. Dracko smirked. "Alternatively, you could have sent them to the feisty Rhinos. The roaches hate them more."

"Too dangerous. And she can't go that far herself."

After lingering around for a while and pestering the critters some more, Dracko's face began melting on one side. Someone had called a road, and he had to oblige. "A road call," he said and thawed.

Moon watched Wu-C2. The Soul Machine seemed to be hung in a vacuum, and its monotony was dampening. Soon exhaustion took over him, and he slumped on the chair.

Meanwhile, far away in the universe, the stars aligned themselves to make way for Wu-C2. A brilliant white stream reflected in her blue eyes. Dodo sat upright and watched the Soul Machine wash in the milky light. A gathering of foggy faces surrounded them: each with two deep silvery eyes sitting loose on long, ancient-looking weathered faces. Big booming sounds blanketed them. The biggest stars made the lowest, most profound sounds, like tubas and double basses, while small stars spoke in high-pitched voices, like celestial flutes. It was a space symphony. Wu-C2 turned on the translator.

A high-bass roar filled Wu-C2's cabin. "Awhh...Not the most opportune moment for a visitor." This probably was the biggest and the oldest star at the far end. He seemed to have some problem with his eyesight and blinked ceaselessly.

"Awhh," he groaned again. "It's been a while since I've exercised my lips to talk. Quite a cumbersome effort, I must say. Now let me see who we have here." He drew nearer and grew in brightness. The Soul Machine was flooded with its brilliant lights. "Hmm...Quite interesting. That seems to be Woozy Do. Moon's girl. The last time he was here, he brought stardust, a precious little gift." His lips made a puckering sound.

Several other stars grew bright in the appreciation of that memory.

Moon sure seemed to be popular here. Wu-C2's human heart felt a tinge of pride rising.

The star spoke slowly again, "I have been watching him, Moon, his notorious plays with the destiny of his own and the remaining few of his kind. That reminds me, are there any left of his kind?"

"Unfounded" said the background voices in unison.

The old Star continued, "He has been brewing trouble for almost a century now. It only stands to reason his mischiefs will come to light one day." He fell silent. "Hmm. Let's see what he has got you into?"

Another star closer to him whispered inaudible gibberish.

The hairy bush-like brows on the older star's face met. "I see. I see. Hmm. Outrageous. Treacherous and foolhardy to get in the way of the roaches."

As the gatekeepers of the world's fate and the guiding lights of the universe, the Stars always took the task of directing travelers to their ultimate aim.

They had been contesting Saros' decision of banning space and time travel, albeit discretely, and cockroaches they openly resented. But even from their standards, the risk was a bit too much this time.

"Moon's girl. We hope you know that the creature you carry with you obliterated your kind." His brows knotted together.

"Obliterated. Input needed," said Wu-C2.

The brows on senior star met severely and he called up an urgent deliberation to debate the ethics and rationale of letting the roach pass along with Wu-C2.

"Honorable members of the celestial community. I call upon you to shine your insights on this dilemma and deliberate the vices and virtues of letting this brave lady pass the space gates. The Star community has always appreciated the curious ones on adventures, and human history shows that we have relentlessly lent our lights to brave hearts. Our efforts have been sincere, and we have forever beckoned the curious. Our Star, North, bears a testament to our copartnery."

The bright star at the far end blinked in agreement.

"Young lady, the Star Community appreciates your appetite for adventure. However, you have fellow traveler, and I'm afraid to say a-not-much-desired presence. A live roach."

The assembly was taken over by whispers, oohs and hmms.

"My fellow stars, considerable is the fact that this here is no ordinary lady. She is Moon's genesis. One of the last remaining hopes for humanity."

Whispers grew.

The old Star spoke again: "Gentlemen, I call your contributions in reasons and resolutions. We have an unprecedented dilemma here. Should we administer the right of this young lady to explore the magnificent secrets of this universe or uphold the rights of the rest universe to secure its safety from future assaults of live cockroaches?"

Anticipating the acuity of the issue at hand, the stars huddled for an urgent discussion.

A weathered star spoke: "However inconsequential, an individual's right is the foundation of the rights of all. Denial to one may imply denial to all."

Another voice contested: "But what about the Star community's commitment to the greater good? By allowing that hideous roach to pass, won't we be dishonouring our peace treaty and jeopardizing the future of the Universe?"

"Oh, that's balderdash. When have we cared? Haven't we witnessed the destruction and revival of things a million times? Attempting to keep things the way they are is all but a futile pursuit. Who knows it better than us? Let the lady exercise her rights, and we'll witness the subsequent development or damage."

The old star moaned and groaned at their arguments. Once the voices settled out of exhaustion, he spoke to Wu-C2 again: "A million years now, and I haven't understood the human ways. It fails our reason why a half-human like you wants to carry something to the future that destroyed the past of your kind."

"Reason. Input needed."

The Star let out an audible sigh. "But humans have always acted against their interests. Out of some temporary whims and childish pride. Hmm." He stared at Wu-C2, and she felt a flutter in her heart.

"Do you have a reason for reviving this roach?"

Sparks rose and flew out of Wu-C2's head, creating a thorny crown of lights over her head.

The old star sighed louder this time, "Just as I thought. You have none. Hmm. Very well. Let the voting commence."

The results were out quick. Twenty-six yes and 39 nos.

"In the interests of the innocent populace of the universe, the Star community has concluded that you must leave the roach where it belongs, i.e., Vespa, and then resume your journey. Considering the perils of the creature, we also prohibit you from going back without forsaking the roach. For Wu-C2, ignorant as you appear to be, you risk losing the creature at an undesirable place in space, jeopardizing the universe's peace. Dangerous as it is, it must be watched at all times."

Sensing the hazard, the Soul Machine hopped parallel to the Starway and back, trying to find a way out.

Wu-C2 said: "Error detected. We were heading toward that orange way, and now we are going away from it. Input: Realign the trajectory."

Where the hell was Bella-Dilla?

A slight crackling sound breezed in from the other side, but the signal was soon lost. That was the thing about Bella-Dilla; the nearer you got, the more you were cut off from the universe. Because it didn't have nodes in time and space, some critics believed it to be the thought domain of the Saros. But that was a made-up excuse because the mercurial temperament of its witches discouraged any kind of inquiry. Bella-Dilla was a portal that opened and closed at the witches' wish.

The Soul Machine moved to-and-fro aimlessly.

But it seemed to be a bit too late already. The Vespian radars had detected unusual commotion around stars and had released emergency fleets. The Stars could now see the swarms of robot cockroaches inching close.

"The roaches are unwelcomed here. To prevent the contamination of the star space, those despicable creatures must be kept at bay at all costs. Therefore, Wu-C2, we urge you to take this unpleasant task upon yourself and deliver the creature to where it belongs."

The brilliance that followed was blinding as stars rearranged themselves and veered to create a longer track to the other side of Bella-Dilla. A great deal of shifting ensued before they straightened up in two straight parallel lines.

And then, right in front, Wu-C2 saw a familiar sight. A giant brilliant red ball was swirling inside fiery rings of blue fire. Though the scene was breathtaking, a sinister feel oozed out of that planet. Dodo climbed up on Woozy's shoulders to get a clearer view.

But the Soul Machine went berserk. It hopped a few stars and nudged the rest to break loose. Wu-C2 noticed the flashing controls in front of her displaying incoherent letters like the fidgety babble of a toddler.

"A malfunction," she said and pushed the buttons to reconnect with Moon. Meanwhile, the machine sidled to get off the trail, but the stars were equally determined to carry out their sentence. The Soul Machine shook and retracted.

Once again, the screen in front lit up. This time sure and crisp. "Warning: you are closing in Vespa. The planet of treacherous robot cockroaches. Reconsider your step forward."

The Soul Machine dialed Moon again. A clatter and mixed shrill sounds of changing frequencies breezed in from the other end. But it was too faint to decipher. Vespa's boom and hiss took over all the other sounds. Wu-C2 amplified the sound on the screen.

Rising and falling at 70 decibels and reaching them at a frequency of 250 hertz, those high and low wheezing sounds were familiar for Wu-C2. "Output. Snore. Inference: Moon has shut himself off to sleep."

Anything under the ambit of the universe knew Vespa. Its deceptive and hostile ways. But Wu-C2 leaned again to read the description:

Vespa: the planet rated most ruthless and unforgiving. Vespa had assaulted almost every other planet except Pleritus and Lucas, the duo it protects. Everyone else is unsought.

Those words dispersed as they had appeared, like fluff, and a new set of words flashed on the screen. "Press blue to continue. Black to escape."

"You must push a button to proceed." The screen beeped again.

Wu-C2 pressed blue.

Rings of blue fire sucked the machine in, and Wu-C2 couldn't see stars anymore. A sea of flames roared all around as far as she could see. They slapped the machine hitting its surface like stones and toppling it like a raging storm. In that heat, the machine's extremities appeared to melt. Wu-C2's human heart overpowered her robot side and throbbed, ready to pounce out of her body.

"Anxiety," she said.

Once inside the Vespian environment, the Soul Machine gained tremendous momentum. With its trajectory pointed to a capsule, the machine was hurtling at severe speed, cutting middle stripes of blues and blacks that were Vespa's days and nights stacked up in layers. Vespa didn't move around any sun. Its sun and the planets stayed at their place, as commanded by it. The Vespian cockroaches, retaining their earthy instincts, preferred still and stale environments. One reason they readily relinquished the far away planet, Lucas, to the animals. The darker, flimsier, and more humid the place, the better it was.

Vespa's night rings were made of enormous floating objects that blocked sunlight and reflected the bulk of it. And the blue twilight rings were made of giant flashlights that surrounded the planet.

The humongous scale of the capsule began to reveal itself. Made of metals that had burned and corroded itself to a rusty gray, it rested on a barren land vacant and flat as far as eyes could see. The Soul Machine hit the ground with a dusty thump. Parked aside the capsule, it now looked like a speck. Its navigation screen was beeping fast: "Warning: Do not step out."

Wu-C2 pulled the roach out from her pocket. Something else dropped: chewing gum.

She cocked her head at the square treat. "A gum."

Moon had shown her how it was to be put in her mouth and grinded leisurely.

"Enter purpose." She had said, and the activity was put off for later.

Back then she had cocked her head once and slid the

gum into her pocket, like she did this time. Completely motionless, the roach now appeared dead to the bone. She dangled it top-down, holding one of its back limbs—still nothing. Dodo, too nudged it with its paw, kneading it and leaving it resembling mush.

Wu-C2 unplugged herself, and the Soul Machine obliged, unfolding its roof like a blooming lotus. Like a freshly hatched chicken, Wu-C2's frame popped from its broken egg shape. A strong smell of rust thrust into her human nose, and the excess humidity accumulated around her, pasting her hair flat on her head. In that deathly silence, she stood baffled, pressing her hands against the shell. Was she to move out or stay? Without Moon's input, she felt wedged into eternal inaction.

She pressed random buttons on the command panel. One in particular released sharp streams of ultrasonic sounds at 40 HZ. Incorporated into the contraption with an intent to detect surrounding impediments, the frequency was also known to affect repulsion among the roaches.

A screeching siren blew as if the whole planet had turned into one big red alert. She pressed her robot hand hard on her human ear and retreated. The Soul Machine's roof shriveled quickly. Wu-C2's human ear kept ringing long after the alarm went off as if it never did. The ground around came alive. What looked like a stagnant barren field rose and fell like cliffs and valleys, wafting the Soul Machine high up and low with it.

But the commotion was nothing against the capsule that was waking up, towering above her, unfolding into a massive metal cephalopod uncurling its giant tentacles that housed many more miniature sleeping robots. Once out, imagination failed to fit those massive objects into their tiny niches. A boom grew.

Everywhere Wu-C2 turned to see, some piece of metal was metamorphosing into a distinct moving creature. The plated ones floated like weightless disks high up in the air while vertical shapes stationed themselves on the ground and reached for the sky. Some stood as tall as the tree houses in Utopia, crossing a dozen nights and days of the Vespian sphere and almost touching its fire rings.

Soon the Soul Machine was standing in a sea of metal forms. The floating plates hovered on top and methodically covered the days above, drowning the space into a dark night. In that darkness, the sounds of metal tinkle, clink, clank, and thuds could be heard ever so clearly. And then there was her heavy breathing making much noise.

She heard the first flutter of the flying roaches. Darting to her from the front and skittering at the sides, they scraped the machine's exteriors with their twitching antennas and limbs. The sound became denser. Wu-C2 made a rough mental estimate of the sounds and estimated at least thousands of them. The hair of her human hand inadvertently stood up.

A streak of light escaped the blanket above, and she felt a sharp stab in her human eye at the sudden outburst. She strained to see the indistinct dark shadows that floated atop. As her eyes accustomed to the flare up, she could see many buggy eyes and knifelike antennas fixated on the machine. Tears ran from her human eye to her chin. The top plate floated off the ceiling, and amid a swarm of flying roaches, a giant tentacle unfurled above. It hung right above the Soul Machine. A dozen smaller tentacles grew and latched themselves on it, arresting it from all sides.

The Soul Machine was hurled high up in the air to what seemed like a monstrous mouth of the cephalopod, a slimy deep black abyss. Dark and humid: a haven for roaches. Once inside the giant's mouth, the fall retarded, and Wu-C2, now that her eyes were accustomed to the darkness again, could see its innards. Much like the abyss she had known, humid and rusty with a disgusting smell that filled your senses and probed your gut to deject all that was inside. Roaches resembling the ones she had with her sat in tiny cubicles embedded in the flushed walls of the bottomless well where Wu-C2's machine was sinking: different hues and shades close to brown, each with half a dozen pointy and squirming limbs. One roach unzipped its stomach to see its gut and innards spilled out. He zipped it back after careful inspection.

Wu-C2 went off in a sleep mode. In her human nightmare, the roach she had crushed sprung back to life. It darted at her from the front and grew and shrank in size. Latching its spiky antennas to her lips, it attempted to crawl up her nose. She thrust it away. It multiplied into thousands of roaches, flitting from all directions and darting toward her, leaving their slimy tracks all over her. Getting crushed and sloshed under her feet as she walked. Wu-C2 hurled them away with swift movements of her arms.

"Are you going to squish me, for I squished one of you?" She said.

Wu-C2 was now hovering over her roach-leaden form. Constricted, bloodied, and dismembered. She watched the roaches slit her head open and extricate bits and pieces out of her, mostly her robotic parts. They slashed her robot arm and stitched another in its place, a human one.

She heard a thud which was followed by a meow. "Dodo."

Wu-C2 switched on again.

Wu-C2 could read the words flashing on the side walls of the innards. "A human. A roach." Things moved lightning fast after that. A quick rewind. Two giant tentacles attached themselves to the machine, and it was hoisted up. They withdrew and hurled the machine into space with a spectacular force, so much that she didn't notice the fire rings this time. The monitor in front of her beeped. "You are now leaving Vespa."

That Vespa released Wu-C2 back in space was no pardon or glitch. The decision came as a ramification of the roaches' discovery of one of them tucked inside Wu-C2's pocket. Their hope was revived: repopulate the Earth under the supervision of roaches and prove their governance superiority over Saros. Wu-C2, a docile non-questioning creature, served as their ideal human sample. The roaches had deactivated her robot side, making her a complete human. Her roach too was alive now.

Back in Utopia, Moon still snored.

Chapter 4: Dazed in the Deadly Lucas

Wu-C2's hands shook, and things looked absurd. Her controls were slower and duller, and she could feel sensations in her robot arm. Unaware that Vespa had activated her fully human form, she wondered at the source of the drift. A virus?

But the true shock was yet to be seen. The roach had sprung into a new life. Its limbs wriggled furiously as it flitted inside the machine crashing against its sides. Dodo was odd too. It hissed and snarled.

The roach reciprocated Wu-C2's feelings. It flapped its wings and settled in the farthest corner constricting itself in a tiny space on the rear deck. They were trapped in that tiny cabin with Dodo baring her teeth now and then. Wu-C2 felt her hands growing cold.

But the Soul Machine wasn't stopping anytime soon. From the scales and the newness of the galaxies, she judged she was way away from the track Moon drew. The stars, too, were receding and diminishing in numbers. Just a handful of them now. The last thread. Nothing beyond them. Or so they said because no one knew. Not even Moon. All they knew of it was an infinite neutral space of gray that swallowed everything into itself, turning it gray and neutral.

Soak, they called it. A big dark riddle for all. Myriad incidents of the greatest and mightiest stars and suns disappearing in that space existed in US-Δ's accounts, and the planets rightly kept their distance. Only Lucas had the mettle to remain near it. "Lucas," Wu-C2 recalled, the world of animals:. Vespa had sent the Soul Machine where it wanted its roach to be.

Wu-C2 picked the shiniest golden gem with silver dots and brought it in front of her eyes. This new sensation swept her off her feet: "You are." She searched for the words "beautiful?". Even Dodo looked so soft, so fluffy. She dropped the gem and pressed it tightly against her chest. Unaccustomed to such abrupt displays of affection, Dodo's system warmed up and a fuse shot in its head.

The distant streaks of yellow and blue were way past them, and only Dodo's eyes and the gems shone. But Wu-C2 was ecstatic. Her human heart was working at 100%. The world had sprung to life, and everything she saw beckoned her to own it. Dodo was hot as a bun, and sparks rose from it often. It purred.

A speck of golden light appeared on the horizon. Behind it sneaked the sparkling blue-green planet of Lucas. As if someone threw a lot of stardust on a gummy cloud and pasted it in place.

Wu-C2 leaned to read the instructions: "Lucas soldiers. Mostly harmless. They believe if you've made it till here, you deserve to get in too."

Inside Lucas, a sheet of fresh rain-washed pastures and radiant green shelterbelt bordered by rusty mountains greeted them. The peaks competed with the lush fields for space, taking them over at places, winning, and outlining the horizon. They rose and fell like thousands of snow-kissed waves rendered golden under the morning sun. Wu-C2 marveled at the brilliance of sparkling golden light that bathed everything.

She looked up at the source of it. The brightest gold ball

fronting a clear blue sky. "What's that? And it is so…It is so…" Wu-C2's words were hung like an old gramophone, and she kept repeating "So..So.". Her gaze was pinned on the most brilliant golden sun. And though it was bright and gold, its light was such that it didn't hurt any naked eye however close or however long they saw it. It just made the looker hungrier.

"So bright. So round. So cool. So warm." Wu-C2 was murmuring in broken words. Her utterances dropped bit by bit like honey dripping from an overflowing beehive. Words flashed on the screen before her: "Warning: Lucas Sun, with magic rays. Do not look at it. Repeat: Do not look at the golden sun. Lethal." Oblivious, Wu-C2 ignored even the twangy sounds the machine made.

Wu-C2 wasn't an exception. Once you had the fortune of watching the Lucas sun, it was the only thing youever wanted to see, and you never got enough of it.

"So bright. So round. So cool. So warm."

The machine was now standing on a massive clearing with tufts of grassy patches raising their heads from all around. Animals big and small huddled close to get the best view of their cherished sun. Giant mammoths, saber-tooth cats, moa, wolves, wallabies, seals, rhinoceros, ceratopsians, ankylosaurs, gorillas, and rabbits all sat dazed, watching the big bright sun. Some emaciated to death, for they seemed to have forgotten to eat.

Back in Utopia, Moon was waking up.

He driveled, "A thousand years..na..na...less..less.. flavorsome anyway". Moon was fond of this hazy ground between wakefulness and sleep. The domain of not belonging neither here nor there. One of the many perks of knowing how to shut his robot side. But this time, his pleasure was short-lived. He was jolted back to wakefulness after a brief look at the screen.

Thrown away from its travel trajectory, the Soul Machine had disappeared from the screen. Its faint beeps flickered from some faraway place.

Moon had to think fast. "Incredible. The Soul Machine can't malfunction. Never strayed from its path. Where could it go?"

He downed a pill to quiet his human heart that fluttered wildly. Quelling the inanity, he checked to the far end on the screen, scanning every planet he had programmed for Wu-C2 to see, but there was no sign of her. He had to expand the view to newer and unmarked places.

"How long was I out?" He almost yelled at the chair that immediately spoke 31 and a quarter mars moon cycles.

Reluctantly he moved signals to all the unplanned places, to the scary corners he feared he should have warned her about. To his temporary respite, Wu-C2 wasn't there.

"Where could they be?"

He peered at the screen. At last, he had to do what he never wanted— extend his search to Vespa and Lucas. The probability of her landing in Vespa was stronger, which wasn't a relief. Her being there would have meant the end of the mission.

Static and hideous Vespa was a bittersweet relief. He zoomed over to see the still capsule. "Lay dead, you monster."

As he pulled closer to Lucas, the signal grew stronger. There he found the Soul Machine parked and Wu-C2 bedazzled. Something was different about her. In the way she hung up at the light, she looked more vulnerable and fragile, clumsy too. Her straight-as-a-stick frame was a bit droopy.

"Outrageous and magnificent."

Moon marveled at Wu-C2's likeliness to him, of landing at all the wrong places at the bad times.

"Can you see that?" He spoke to the chair. "Why she is repeating my mistakes. Incredible."

As he zoomed closer, he noticed something uncanny. Her eyes were tearing up out of exhaustion. A robot eye could well bear that strain. Was something wrong with her systems? To him, Wu-C2 was still a cyborg, immune to any magic or space hypnosis.

Moon tabled the query for later. The bigger challenge was to pull her back. Was he to call Dracko, like he did the last time when he got stuck? But to do so, he had to explain to Dracko how she landed there in the first place. Moon had kept his naps a secret indulgence for long.

Wu-C2 sat still, almost like a picture.

He moved closer to the screen, so close that his breath built haze over it. And traced his wrinkled human fingers on the screen, on Wu-C2's face, and then to the light where it was the brightest. His brows met as he said with pressed lips, "the dreadful sun."

Wu-C2 was stuck in a limbo of stupefied, never moving things.

Moon weighed the possibilities by engaging his predictions and memories. "But it can't travel that far."

He counted on his fingers and mumbled indistinct words again, downing another pill. He paused and counted, sometimes beginning all over again.

It wasn't that he didn't resent dozing off at all wrong times. But a big part of becoming an adult is learning to forgive oneself for the same mistake over and over again.

"Can't be the machine's work." Once again, he moved closer to the screen and stared at it for a long time, making an enormous effort to avoid any contact with the sun's brilliance, even the reflected one that shone on Wu-C2's face. The pull was intense, like a mega magnet for his human side.

After spending three mars days on the thinking task, Moon realized that his only hope was the machine. Inbuilt with eons of data and situation simulations, it was the most suspicious and above any influence. And so, he decided to make contact. On this unguarded frequency path, this was the most lethal thing to do and could put them all right on G-4's and roaches'radar, but then he was short of choice.

Soon he was sending frequencies. This time more intense, more detectable. And as if the machine had been waiting for it, it caught them on the first strike. "You must move out now. Move out of Lucas. Now! Trace the new track." All at once, the Machine started gearing up.

Moon's fears were real. His signals were captured on the G-4's and cockroaches' radar. "Singular contact detected." Troops were activated at both places, tracking the source and receiver of transmission.

The Soul Machine was still glued to the Lucas ground when Moon heard a thump. From the look of it, it was pinned under something heavy. The impact was such that it sagged in the middle, its roof almost touching Wu-C2's head. Moon looked closely. "What." The effort to keep his eyes away from the Lucas Sun was overwhelming. Water oozed from his human eye in persistent streams. He rubbed it with his fingers and slapped his human side to crush any sluggishness left.

"Move from that place. Now!" He repeated.

The machine made various sounds and then switched on the blinkers that were its call for help.

Moon stared at the blinking screen. The machine's ceiling sagged a bit more. By now, Wu-C2's eyes were blood red with exhaustion.

"Let's try...Try and see if somebody or something is moving up here."

The machine unfolded its view screens to 360 degrees. Dazzling as the Lucas sun, the first look revealed a hundred thousand stupefied creatures in all shapes and sizes surrounding the machine. Many, the last time he knew of them, were extinct. It was hope served with dashes of despair. Because nothing moved. Once extinct on Earth, these precious creatures were getting wasted again.

"See again," He commanded. How he wanted to see these creatures up close and appreciate their peculiarities but had no time in hand.

Moon's eye itched and burned now.

The G-4 had begun his hunt. Hundreds of Ψs flew out of Utopia, tracing the recipient of the frequency and scattering out into space. The Vespians, too, sent their roaches. But instead, in the direction of the transmitter, i.e., to Utopia to investigate the source of the call. They had two reasons. First, the roaches had always been suspicious of cyborgs and needed little reason to probe their planet. Second, Lucas was distant and hence cumbersome to probe, and then there were those Rhinos.

In no time, the cockroaches were hovering over the Utopian skies, checking the cyborgs and stopping the robots. Perched up on his tower and riveted to his screen, G-4 monitored these advances. His tentacles sprawled all around him and reached up to the extremities of the control room, a few dangling from the observatory's fenestrations. They made room for the roaches to sneak inside. Releasing their gunky glue in copious amounts and pasting the G-4's arms to the tower's profile, they restrained any movement and paralyzed him temporarily.

Then they scuttled to the corners and into the crevices of the monitors. This was where they interrogated the UE-Δs. Utopia's big secret wasn't a secret anymore. The exposure shamed potato-shaped UE-Δs, who were forced to move from their perennial sits. They went red in the face, supple in their stance and wobbly in their legs. The roaches ran through Utopia's systems, checking every detail and input and copying its secret cyborg data by dozens.

For G-4, this scrutiny was a question on his authority and competence. His limbs were stuck to the disgraceful glue long after the roaches flew back, barely giving him any attention. In an unprecedented rebuttal that followed the cockroaches' departure, his arms unfurled and released the million mini soldiers in them.

Not too far away, with one view fixed on the ψs and other on the roaches, Moon carefully ducked the investigation. His focal point of interest were the Lucas animals. "So alive and so dead. Shouldn't be."

A dust storm grew on the horizon of Lucas enveloping

everything in the vicinity. Moon couldn't see the animals anymore. Then came a thud flinging the machine off the ground, many miles up in the air. Right when it was about to touch the ground, another thud came, and it was back up high in the air. As unfortunate as the event may look, it woke Wu-C2 up.

Her eyes felt hot and the tears accumulated in them, blurring everything.

"Wake up, Woozy Do." Moon's voice breezed in. "And close your eyes for human's sake."

Wu-C2's chest hurt as she breathed air into her human lungs after a long time. She sat erect.

"That's better. Now, I want you to do as I say. Move your hands to the front, a little left now." Open the top cabinet. Yes, right, that one. Now take those glasses and wear them."

Wu-C2's eyes eased when she wore those thick glasses. Pitch black with many coatings of gold, the shades offered total protection from Lucas' rays.

As expected as this relief was, Moon knew that at the rate the Lucas Sun was burning, it was losing its luminance with time. The same glasses wouldn't have worked a few centuries back.

"Now. Look out and tell me what you see."

Wu-C2 held the dashboard with one hand and her seat with the other and propped herself up to look outside. Various aches and pains she hadn't known in her Utopian form appeared. Once again, she wondered about the virus. She sidled the thought for later and peered from high up in the air. The machine was up in free flight. Down below stuffed, thick armored four-legged animals chased the machine. With a horn perched on their protruding noses, they charged wayward ruffling everything underneath and around. The ground shook as they ran crushing enchanted tiny beings and toppling the rest. They caught up with the machine upon its descent, kicking it from their stump-like leg, a sharp thrust propelling it further higher up. Wu-C2 lost her grip and dropped on her seat. She rose again to see. This time from the other side. "The creatures. They are kicking us."

Wu-C2 turned the screen 180 degrees to face the front.

"A body armor and sharp snout. And they are wearing glasses, like mine, too."

A guffaw surprised her. "Hohoho. Hohoho. Rascal Rhinos. I thought they left Lucas for good. And it looks like they are having a good time too. Hohoho."

Decedents of their Earthian ancestors, Rhinos choose to concentrate their AI upgrades on physical prowess only. They did not learn to speak but gained fifty times their Earthian might in the form of giant iron-like muscles.

Acclaimed as the Dons of the space, the Rhinos had the reputation of stomping and kicking all that came in their way. Not that they meant any harm. Joust was their idea of life. Many centuries back, the roaring young Lucas Sun had driven them away, and they had retreated to the remote and dark jungles of Pleritus. Havoc ensued in the planet of unexcitable resting trees, and they bemoaned their fate. The dislike was mutual. Rhinos denounced the trees, stamping them with the term "as-good-as-dead and hardly alive." The matter was taken over to Saros, but duty called, and the Rhinos reappeared in Lucas wearing the shades that were Moon's gift to them. Those were the days when Moon and the Rhinos appreciated their outrageous taste of adventure and slipped favors among them.

Since their arrival, they had kicked dozens of dazed Lucas creatures and brought them back to their senses. This feat earned them respect and admiration, even from Saros. Moon looked around for a sign of the Chief Rhino, his champ. But he wasn't to be found, which wasn't a surprise for his tribe had the tendency to stray. One reason they were decimated to a few thousand from a clan of over one million. But even in these small numbers, they were mighty enough to take over any army.

Moon's glee was perplexing for Wu-C2, who was still trying to find her balance inside the rocky machine. Her hand hit Dodo and threw him off his seat, which also woke him up. And then she heard louder thumps shaking the ground evermore. A gigantic version of the animal appeared through the dust cloud, possibly the mother of them all. She came alongside, nudging the smaller ones and driving them away with her grunts and hoofs. As she traced the machine with her snout, Wu-C2 noticed those nostrils were as big as the Soul Machine. She sniffed, and strong gusts of air uprooted the machine from its perch.

"Hit it on its mouth," Moon commanded.

The machine floated up and thrust on the creature's face. It angered the giant who sniffed and huffed. Thumping its legs and retracting, it raised a thick cloud of dust after itself. The retreat was short-lived. Wu-C2 heard thuds again, louder and faster this time. And soon, the machine was charging in the air, kicked far into space by the elephantine Rhino. This time the Soul Machine took its clue and shot off. The rhino kids ruefully watched their toy being tossed into space. With the Soul Machine disappearing in clouds, they followed their mother creating disappointed grunts and making do with kicking their acquainted toys, the stupefied creatures.

Lucas and its sun were left behind. The machine was back in space propelling straight into the infinite darkness.

Something else that neither Wu-C2 nor Moon knew happened. Something fantastic. In their kicks and thuds, the Rhinos had loosened up trackers that Vespa had installed on the machine. Now those lay dead covered in dust and crushed under their feet. In Vespa, the monitors went blank.

With no Vespa force to propel the machine, Wu-C2 soon found herself hanging in a vacuum.

"Decision time. Tell me, Woozy Do, where would you like to go?"

Moon had calculations going on in his head too. With Vespa on the hunt and the G-4 collecting breadcrumbs, he had to hide the Soul Machine somewhere safe. A place out of the Vespa's radar. And there was only one.

"Umm. I guess I know a place like that. Hmm. Yes, you would like to be the brave girl you are." He paused and said, "Over to Bella-Dilla."

Chapter 5: Bella-Dilla

But the bigger question was- Was Bella Dilla going to accept the Soul Machine? For the witches were infamous for their impulse and hard-headedness. And even if they took her in, how long before they decided to gobble her up, being the cannibals they were?

If Moon had known that Wu-C2 had turned into a human before entering that space, the thought would've been cut out of his list. On the contrary, he would have shielded her. But unaware of Vespa's trick, he carried on with his plans.

Bella Dilla — The sticky place. Like some kind of loose glue. The machine made sounds "Plop. plop. squelch," nudging its way into it.

Nasty noises drew around them, growing into giggles as they neared.

Soon they were overpowering: whispers, screeches, laughs and snores. Too many for Wu-C2 to focus on a single one.

"You are in Bella-Dilla now. Neither a planet nor a no-planet. The ancient realm of the modern-day witches."

At the time, when the universe was reshuffling itself, creating newer avenues and discarding its past, Bella-Dilla witches decided to stay as they were, ancient and in love with themselves. They defended their passion for magic like a mother defends her newborn.

A planet that was diametrically opposite to all it was, Vespa dismissed the witches because it couldn't decode their unpredictability. This planet didn't have a form and appeared and disappeared at its will, more on unfounded hunches. One thriving on the fringes of obsolete wasn't worth the trouble of inquiry. The word was: cockroaches were convinced Bella-Dilla would die its death of inanity.

The giggling voices were now crooning nearer. And through the fading mist, the singsong voices came breezing in. Witches were stunned to locate an intruder that was the Soul Machine, and their giggles turned into heart-numbing screeches. Their distaste compounded when Wu-C2's profile appeared out of the mist and their sneers turned into deep distrustful frowns. Bella-Dilla didn't appreciate uninvited guests. Especially so if they were unsightly cockroaches. Next on its list were cyborgs.

But as the sight became more evident and witches came to smell the human odor wafting out of Wu-C2, their demeanor took a u-turn, and their song turned sweet.

A gush of cool wind raised Wu-C2's hair and enveloped her like a cocoon. With tickles all over, she felt funny.

A coarse singsong voice breezed in. "A human. Interesting. It's been a long I've seen one." Many high-pitched chuckles followed, punctuated by an old woman's frantic laughter. The tickles came mixed with pinches that grew sharper now.

"And what must a human do in Bella-Dilla? Enticed by death. Eh? Or is someone so chivalrous to treat us at this odd hour?"

A wrinkled hand appeared from the mist and grabbed Wu-C2's hair, tugging them twice. She could hear a whisper close, almost a whiff over her ear: "Umm. Soft and alive. Warm blood running through supple veins. Young and innocent. Could it be tasty too?"

Another husky voice slapped, "No wicked Bizzy; you must wait."

The high-pitched voice pleaded in return: "But Bizzy is hungry. Bizzy has not eaten live and squirmy human for many hundred years. You said they were gone. You tricked poor Bizzy. Bizzy is pleading now."

"Baloney. Didn't you get a hand sometime back? So juicy. You nibbled on it, like a silly fat witch that you are."

Witches shrieked.

Bizzy screeched. "It was horrible, a rotten piece. Full of hatred. No love juice for Bizzy." She was sobbing now. "Bizzy always gets the thrown-away pieces. Yes. The worst ones. With no feel. This time Bizzy wants the heart. Bizzy wants to eat the feel beating heart. Yes, huff. Huff. Bizzy wants it this time. Bizzy will get it this time."

A series of exclamations and rebukes rained: "Ohhh... what...Heart..No...That's too much to ask. She has lost it."

"Lost it. Lost it. Silly Bizzy. Have you lost it? No one but she gets the heart".

Dodo nestled beside Wu-C2. "What's happening, Dodo?" Wu-C2 whispered. "You can't hear them. Can you?"

The voices grew into growls, cries, and screeches, rendering Wu-C2's ears red hot. Though she sealed them with her hands, they now drummed inside her head, pounding like a hammer. A thousand sounds of many tones and frequencies rising and falling simultaneously.

Wu-C2's hair stood up like thirsty tufts on a dry day. She felt a chill run through her spine, and blood rushed to her head.

Those who knew the ways of the witches could tell they were banishing the human soul from her.

Cocooned inside a blue fog, Wu-C2 was drowsy. The horrific sounds weren't so unpleasant now. With every passing note, they seemed gentler and more rhythmic to her and soon turned into the sweetest lullaby.

"Woo...waah..ri...ra...rum"

The Soul Machine's screen was flickering. "The phantom song. A song of demise, of the death of the human soul." To Wu-C2, who by now was in another realm, it had turned into the sweet song of mother she never had. And she clung to it, hunkering for more.

"Travel. Travel. Travel.

To your darkest dreams.

Travel to never return

to the worlds of neither living nor dead.

To the forever stillness.

And eternal sweet sleep.

Travel, Travel, Travel

travel, never to come back.

Woo..ra. ri. rum."

Wu-C2's eyes were heavy, never blinking, blue and still. Her lips were humming the phantom song "Wooh. Woo. Ra. Ri. Rum.……hmm. hmm. hmm. hmm. Travel, Travel, Travel."

She rolled to the grey-blue fog in the heart of Soak, the giant black hole. Like the witches, Soak, too, was dried for visits. And it prepared itself to assimilate Wu-C2 once and forever.

"Oh sweet human..hmm...hmm...hmm...hmm."

The mist around the Soul Machine cleared and Moon could see Dodo napping. Wu-C2 had disappeared, and a blue fog floated in her place.

"Why? Have they change to reduced their appetite to cyborgs now?"

Moon tried to make sense of it. The witches who had spared him so easily weren't so kind on Wu-C2. Why?

Far away from him, in a parallel universe, Wu-C2 rolled. Her eyes never blinking, her human heart not beating, just her lips humming along with the witches:

Travel to your darkest dreams.

Meanwhile, the cockroaches were getting more and more irked by sure evidence of a Utopian presence in the frequency breach. Impatient and forever scuttling as they were, they bypassed the tracks of the Machine and couldn't find anything substantial. Moon's soldier ants had nibbled on his tracks, and the cockroaches were unwilling to follow Wu-C2's breadcrumbs. An important pretext of it being those crumbs were leading to Bella-Dilla. And the roach theory was: those witches were a bit too much to understand. Better ignore than feel inadequate.

But then something had to be done. Someone had to be accountable. From the deftness of the execution and the involvement of intricate operational know-how, the cockroaches concluded the conspiracy wasn't of a single entity but of the planet as a whole. At the foundation of their suspicion was their perceived deceptional tendency of humans: cyborgs or otherwise.

Now that they had their hypothesis, the violation was to

be punished and was to be punished severely, for they have to live up to their reputation of showing no mercy. So, in droves, they marched to Utopia.

Disciplining Utopia was to be done in stages. The strategy was set: take the guard planets first, disrupt the planet's operations, and most importantly, cut off its energy source, the Utopian sun. In no time, the command was up. A million roaches of various sizes swarmed the red planet, Utopia, covering it from all sides. They tucked their legs and spread their wings weaving a black blanket to block its sun, so not even a spark could find its way into the caged ball inside.

If there was one point where the ways of thinking of Moon and Vespa converged, it was their judgment of each other's motivations. Moon knew the way Vespa dealt with detractors. If they found out what Moon was up to, they would have exterminated everything straight ahead. When he saw the cockroaches approaching, he consulted Dracko.

"Where from here?"

The hologram wavered, "My friend Moon, I'd doubt your judgment if you are anywhere near concluding that those dumb roaches are going to trace back a link to you anytime soon."

Moon threw his head back slightly and studied Dracko casting a lowered gaze on him. "Exactly the mistake mankind did. They underestimated the power of stupidity in great numbers. You know what happened to them."

Unwilling to take any periculous chances, Moon decided to migrate his operations to Earth in a jiffy. The chamber and all.

Using an atom delimiter, he broke the chamber and the chair into atomic parts and packed them in a small condensed ball that could fit in his pocket. While the cockroaches were busy constricting G-4 in his tower, he flew out of Utopia, leaving Dracko behind to cover up for him, as he had done earlier on so many other occasions.

In Bella- Dilla, Wu-C2 was about to enter Soak, the big black hole. The baby gem in Wu-C2's pocket grew colder. It shrank, slipped out from her pocket, and floated in front of her eyes. In it, remnants of Utopia shone ever so clearly. The darker Utopia got, the brighter the gem shone.

By now, Wu-C2's eyes were pitch black — the color of the non-living, a reflection of Soak — not indicating any notice of the spectacle in front of them whatsoever.

The gem floated close to her eyes, and a dim residual spark twinkled weakly in them. From here, the light from the gem registered in her eyes and hit her heart, nudging it to beat a few times.

Her stare riveted on the gem, and she paused her singing. "Moon," she mumbled. The frozen black river in her eyes melted back in blue. A sharp pain stabbed her heart, and she heaved, seething with the sudden air that now puffed up her lungs. Boomerang. She was sucked back into Bella-Dilla. The witches' song sounded unbearably gross this time, like the far cry of a distressed child. The gem was all black by swallowing the darkness of Wu-C2. She found herself in her human body inside the Soul Machine, and the blue fog melted on Moon's screen.

The rebound created ruckus among the witches who retreated briefly for an urgent deliberation.

But Bella-Dilla wasn't leaving Wu-C2 so easily. She could see them: brilliant honey-voiced damsels perched up on their hair dryers, showering right swipes from their long-manicured fingers. Their song dissolved like sweet cotton candy in Wu-C2's ears, fresh like forest birds chirping in an early spring morning.

When they saw Wu-C2 drowsy with her disheveled demeanor, they rolled their eyes and puffed their cheeks. And they sang:

"In a Universe of pretty and sure

the old and ugly desert to die."

Seventy sisters and their furry mongooses made their debut. Their gowns swept the scene as they rode far and near, up and down, toward and away, and their critters adorned with silver necklaces squeaked and swept the way with their big long bushy tails.

The witches huddled around Wu-C2, up close, almost touching her like the nudge of a feather, and squeaked at her look.

"Strange unkempt witch."

Unseemly and unbearable as her sight was, the most urgent task for them was fixing Wu-C2's hair and rouging her bland cheeks.

They caught her by her shoulders and said, "Umm... dreamy..dreamy.. very dreamy" and shook her to dispel any trace of sluggishness.

"Hi.hi.hi..Ho.ho.ho..Quite better. Still not awake." They shook her again. Her arms and legs were shaking vigorously along with their bells and bangles. Shimmer spread all around.

"Where's your kind, strange witch."

To appear awake and sidestep all this shaking, Wu-C2 stretched her eyes as much as she could, almost to the point of pain.

That's when she flew in. The Queen of Zushh. Perched over a massive red hair dryer with her head high and a faraway look in her brilliant eyes that made the present moment seem insignificant, she motioned in graceful slow gestures. Her right swipes were fewer, and her mongoose was bigger, flatter, and fluffier. The creature flaunted a pearled purple collar in brisk gaits. A bunch of witches trailed after her.

When she halted, the mongoose behind her, who wasn't attentive, crashed into her.

"Would you...Behave yourself." She stumbled and straightened her satin dress, casting an apologetic glance at Wu-C2.

Visibly embarrassed with her cheeks turning blood red, she exhaled. "Hey there, hello from the Queen of Zushh. They still call it Bella-Dilla, but what do we have to do with those gross unkempt witches? It would be unfair to call them witches. Rogues they are. If you've met them," she scanned Wu-C2's face fleetingly, and then, almost realizing in an instant, she ordered her mongoose, "Point to be noted. The wild ones shouldn't be allowed to call themselves witches. It is a disgrace."

A dump of likes rained after her and she heaved a sigh of satisfaction.

The witches peered at her with expecting dramatic eyes. A twinkle of envy and admiration in them.

She rolled her eyes up and drawled: "Oh, come on. Give

it up. You can never be like me."

"But we've had our share of spats with them." An apprehensive young witch said, resuming the topic of sharing the "witch" name.

"Now. Did we?" She surveyed the scene with swift dives and nodded to her mongoose. A look of appreciation sneaked in her eyes. That the cannibals spared Wu-C2 was a good enough reason for respect. A smaller bland dryer floated in front of Wu-C2.

"There. Ride it." Drawled the Queen. Her long-lashed eyes flickered.

Wu-C2 tried to make sense of her words.

"Come on, quick. Hop on and lead. You've earned it. All witches deserve a dryer. They deserve the best curls and hair in place."

Wu-C2 looked at the witches and then at the dryer. She cleared her throat. "I...I can't."

A tiny furrow appeared between the Queen's brows.

"What do you mean you can't?"

"I...I don't know how to ride…this."

Gossips crept. "What? Can't ride a dryer? Is that even possible, or might she be distracting?"

"Maybe she wants an upgraded version."

Soon as it was said, the dryer dispersed, and another bigger, shinier one took its place.

"If so, you wish. That's the latest Versace model." The Queen shrugged and said almost dismissively, presenting her forgiving smile again.

Wu-C2 saw the gadget from the corner of her eyes. "I...I

mean, I can't ride this or any. Never done before."

A riot of exclamations ensued.

The sisters, who watched her intently, giggled and resumed their gossips, murmuring skepticisms. "Now that's a truly strange witch."

The revelation was incredible for the Queen. A witch who couldn't ride a dryer was a scandal. Her lips furled in disgust. "What's that smell?"

She looked after Wu-C2 at the Soul Machine. "Something nasty in there."

Her eyes met her wise-looking mongoose. "Are those cockroaches up to some mischief again?"

The mongoose peered at Wu-C2 from under his glasses and then at the machine. "Cockroaches in Bella-Dilla. Looks unlikely to me, my lady."

"Huh. Assured, she returned her attention to Wu-C2. "Fascinating. A witch that can't ride a dryer. How have you survived, and what's that ugly thing you are riding? It is so ancient."

Her chatter was cut by a familiar nasty voice of the old cannibal witch, who having returned from deliberations, whispered.

"That ain't a witch, you naif. That's a human. A one hundred percent human. That we found her first. And that you've left no taste of love, you pass her to us. Hi. Hi. Hi. Juicy so sweet."

The wild witches joined her cackle. "Hi. Hi. Hi. A supposed Queen who can't know food from folks."

A dark shadow grew over the Queen's head. Heavy like a rain-loaded cloud on a stormy day. It sprawled over and rendered the space black, "I say we have stopped eating the living. Makes for a nasty looking sight."

Screeching laughter followed, which was echoed by other witches. "Silly Marissa. What's a witch without a taste of blood? The cockroaches are coming for us all. Where will you go, Marissa? There's no place to go. Have a juicy treat while you still have your freedom."

The voices were cajoling, almost speaking in Wu-C2's ears. Her hair ruffled up by their breath. "Human. You've riled Soak. It wants you back." Wu-C2 could feel the chill surrounding the gathering from all ends.

The Queen glared at her mongoose as if all this mess was his fault, and he looked away. Was it not that she created a separate clear space Zushh on the fringes of Bella-Dilla to keep the wild witches at bay? They were wild and despicable, and though the two clans shared their ancestors, she wanted to do nothing with them. Their reputation was dented, and they received no likes or hearts or support for that matter. But here, she was forced to talk to them.

"The cockroaches won't dare to enter Zushh. Have you forgotten that they haven't for a million years?"

The old witch uttered bone-chilling laughter that cut through her talk: "Silly, Marissa. Times always change. Your human here has already got one. How soon before the rest arrive."

The Queen could have brushed the revelation off but for the smell. She knew there was a trace of truth in the old witches' words.

Hungry Bizzy, who couldn't take it anymore, trailed her hand over Wu-C2's arms. "Bizzy is dying to get some love juice."

The Queen's voice slapped like thunder: "I said no blood!" And with that, a bolt of lightning struck Bizzy. Her straggly hair was set on fire, and her frame was now visible to Wu-C2's naked eye. Emaciated and crouched on her four limbs, with her eyes protruding from her bony cheeks, she was half the size of the Queen and looked almost like an earthly dog.

But contrary to acting as a deterrence, the attack emboldened her. She pounced closer to Wu-C2, and the wild witches behind her began salivating. The Queen had to jump between Wu-C2 and the witches. The seventy sisters did their bit by darting straight into the cannibals and hurling them away with the hot air from their dryers. Soon, the vacuum was torched by lightning flashes and burning wild witches.

Wu-C2 closed her eyes to escape the wash of white. When she opened them, the blue fog of Bella-Dilla had shrunk to a dot, and she was spewed out of it. The Queen's mongoose parked by her side.

He licked his paws indifferently as if the incidence was the most ordinary one. "As if you had never seen a mongoose before." He said, visibly offended by Wu-C2's inadvertent stare. "I must tell you that this ignorance is quite demeaning at my age of respect and recognition. To be more accurate, I find it on the meaner side as if you pretend not to know me and be someone else than yourself for some quaint reason. And I may have to go to the extent that you want to disregard my accomplishments, as great as they were so that you can look me in the eye, just like you do at those undistinguished wild ones."

Wu-C2 averted her eyes.

"Who is she?" she said.

The mongoose jumped in surprise: "That's the most audacious question I have heard. I must insist that this is beyond audacious. Slander against the beloved Queen of Zushh?" He said, fixing his contentious eyes on Wu-C2 and clearing his throat: "Beloved Queen of Zushhh. The most beloved of all. You can trust my word for as prestigious as I am, I have traveled the whole universe before gaining the most respectful position of a luminary." His gaze remained intact at Wu-C2 until she nodded. Then he looked around, craning his neck to be sure, and said in a whisper: "And though I find this work unmerited considering the qualities such as mine, you know, I do it for the sake of Zushh, the only beloved space that exists in a hateful universe under the shadow of Vespa. That makes me remember, oh, how terrible it is. Terrible. Too terrible." He shrugged his head and looked at Wu-C2, a tiny flicker of condescendence in his look. "My name is Zu, the keeper of Zushh." He heaved, frowned, and looked at her from the corners of his eyes. "Makes me wonder how come you haven't heard it."

Wu-C2 didn't venture to contradict him this time and nodded fast to avert his stare. He cleared his throat again and spoke with a streak of excitement, "Knew it. Knew you must have been ridiculous on purpose."

The frown on his face dissolved. "So where were we? Oh Yes. The Beloved Queen of Zushh. Long long back. Longer than the time itself, there was a mighty black hole. You wouldn't have seen a black hole as mightier. Cockroaches claimed its ownership, and it swallowed great parts of the universe, dogged to render everything else black. The

   Wu-C2

purest black, the black of hatred. Soak, it was called. And it swallowed everything, even your shiny stars. Would you believe that? Hmm. Unfortunately, it fathomed the courage to steer to our beloved Queens. Big mistake. That's when our beloved Queens shone the brightest and hemmed the darkness to where it belonged. Now they fly on their dryers, light the dark skies, and wake up sleepy people..Umm..such as you." He heaved and wiped tears of gratitude from his eyes. A realization dawned upon him, and he made a futile attempt to undo what he had done. "And knowing this is the biggest secret of the universe, I suppose you'd keep itself to you?"

He gave Wu-C2 a suspicious stare.

"Yes. Yes. Of course", Wu-C2 said.

Knowing the hazard of sticking around Wu-C2 and spilling more such secrets of Zushh, he decided to leave immediately. He dispersed like the fluff he had come with.

Wu-C2 was now out of Bella-Dilla, in the open. Exposed to be tracked again.

Chapter 6: Braving up for the battle ahead

"Goddamn witches will always be witches," grunted Moon sitting atop a pile of metal junk and massive voids oozing gunk. Earth, however, devastated and dreadful it had become, still felt like home. His chamber, too, looked better here, fitting like a glove in the chaos, as it had always belonged to this place with all its weird creepy crawlies that flit stronger under the sunlight. Like someone had breathed a new life in them. They quickly huddled in the sunlit corners. Moon was amazed at the thinnest creatures' ability to retain their oldest evolution memories.

In Utopia, in place of his bunker, now a huge vacuum stood, his dwelling wolfed up by soldier ants. There was no going back. Not that he had any plans to return, not so soon. Moon momentarily shut his robot side and stuffed his human lung with air. It was a suicidal act. Under the influence of gravity, he was now aging way faster. The extra oxygen rusted his parts sooner than thought. Tufts of grey hair shot up at unexpected places on his face and limbs. And a tiny wrinkle marched onwards from the corner of his human eye, and he looked older in a matter of few moments.

At some distance, the chair, now transformed into a high one-eyed pillar, had landed just the right spot for them to park. Its aids soldier ants were drilling next to the turf of an active volcano. This place, spiking up from the surrounding lands at an unprecedented slope, was to function as an observatory, a watchtower for the surrounding sea and grounds to the far end. Its volcanoes were the perfect camouflage with their incessant hiss, booms, and bangs. Happening, Moon had called it. Even the sea, too, could give shelter in urgency. The chair had worked it all up. Terrific job. If only Dracko could see it too. He had always appreciated the random acts of intelligence. But then, the acquaintance between Moon and the chair was longer than his relationship with Dracko. And he shared some secrets with the chair too.

The Earth that Moon saw was a dystopian version of the Earth he had known from his records and time travels. He couldn't but feel sorry for how it had turned out. Away from its pleasant warmth, it was now a hub of extremes: extreme heat, extreme cold, extreme natural disasters, and extreme hostility, a dump yard for Vespa.

Moon refocused on the chair, quite satisfied with its progress. They had landed safely on Earth and found the perfect spot. But it wasn't just her working brilliantly. The robot ants were out in space, too, at work again. Nibbling on the traces of the Soul Machine's trails as it hopped galaxies. Moon knew this would do for the time being, but sooner or later, the G-4, with a similar and bigger army of his own, would get to it. He had to find another way out, and soon.

The volcano erupted again, disrupting his thoughts, and he had to switch his robot side on while scooting to the chair. The human part in him felt delighted seeing the drowning, floating, and melting metal debris. Contrary to what the G-4 calimed, those things weren't unperishable. "Haa. He claimed Earth was destroyed forever. Let him see now." Moon said out loud. A few patches of cooled and hardened virgin ashen blue magma made him ecstatic. And for a fragment of a second, he thought the impossible: "Earth: she is still alive. Could we go back and rebuild what we lost? Turn the time around?" he sighed.

Another bout of wishful thinking. He looked at the

sea swarming up with scrap—the surviving creatures in it murderous with their coping mechanisms. Moon watched them gobble up those hard tin cans. They seemed at home in the acidic river environment, jumping and rolling to snap at the hardest metal, as if it was the most ordinary thing to do. Earth had forever been known for its resilience and power to fall and rise — to almost die and rebound to a fuller and stronger life again. Often deadlier. He knew those creatures were gaining control steadily and silently in those bottomless depths. Rebuilding themselves and in what way? "Vespa must start counting its days too." Somewhere this destruction made him happy. Anything with a beating heart was a better ruler than switches and signals, murderous or not. He was delighted at the thought.

Back in Utopia, the Vespian cockroaches were hijacking the utopian skies. Massive giant ones were seen flying along with scooters and the shoots. The big ones crushed the capsules, and roads crashed and crumbled in them. Heaps of ψs lay entangled by the roadsides. Once prided, the Utopian systems were falling fast like a house of cards. Much to awaken the ire of both G-4 and Dracko. Dracko looked up at the darkened skies and frowned ever so deeply.

He hovered over the clusters of cockroaches in an attempt to reason with them. But seeing the ventral view of an overturned roach, he sneered, "Man, you sure look gross," and stepped back.

He rotated his roads upright, blocking the way to G-4's tower. Not that he wanted to protect G-4, but just so that was where the cockroaches wanted to reach. And anything that the cockroaches wanted, he was determined to deduct. The cockroaches latched themselves to the standing roads in swathes and exerted their entire force to bring them down. The roads buckled under pressure but didn't lose their ground. It was a stalemate. The cockroaches got stalled, keeping them pinned.

"Not too smart, are you?" Dracko sneered.

Bigger trouble was looming for Utopia. The big roaches seemed only a scab in front of the little ones. High up in the sky, the tinier ones were weaving a blanket, locking their limbs with one another. A shadow engulfed the planet, disconnecting it from its sun and the rest of the universe. Like Earth, Utopia's sun was the sole source of its energy.

Perched up on his 80 miles tall metal observatory, G-4 watched the rumpus down below on magnifying screens. Utopia shared its resemblance with the last battleground he saw on Earth. He watched roads lifting up and down and Dracko dancing above them amidst cockroaches. The sight of disorderly Dracko had always been unpleasant to him; something was menacing about that absurd face, something so human. He had always known it but could never trace it back to its roots. But today, unexpectedly, that hologram seemed to be his only ally.

His dissatisfaction was compounded, and an utter disgust crept into his veins when he saw cyborgs being chased by roaches. It wasn't routine supervision. Vespa was treating Utopia like an aberration, containing it on all fronts. G-4 needed to escape. This was his last chance. If at all, he was to prove his innocence and worth to Saros. The last time those cockroaches had swallowed a planet, it was erased forever from the Universe's memory. He had to move. This secret escape and abandonment of his planet, his command, made the 1 percent human in him mortified. And a 100 percent of him wanted a resolution this time, human or not. Seven hundred fifty years of his efforts were drowned in a drain. It would be another century before Utopia could be free again from Vespian commands, if ever. Someone had to pay.

With massive blows from a giant metal saw, he hacked himself into two. Each part with an arm, eye, ear, leg, and halved torso. He was to explode again if needed. For now, his parts were to go to Pleritus and Earth. The human in him knew those were the only two wild places where chaos could have bred and survived. That blue-green planet, Earth, Vespa must have obliterated it way back. It was no good in the Universe order. Why they were making Utopia pay? Vespa was wrong. But that was the thing with the cockroaches. They couldn't reason. They wanted a formulaic universe, even at the cost of no universe. They had kept Earth to dump their debris. Contradicting the cockroaches was out of the question. His only option was to flee, find the source of menace, and bring Utopia to justice.

G-4 flew out of Utopia, deserting the planet scrambling for light and air, buried under the massive hive of flitting cockroaches. They were scuttling over his tower, skidding into the shadowy corners, for more horror of US-Δs and leaving grime everywhere. A handful of Σscleaning after them. It was the first time for many things: exposed and disgraced, the topmost ten massive-headed potato-shaped US-Δs were seen following G-4 out in space. Before leaving, they ordered Ψs a real spy job to track Moon and Wu-C2. And the Σs took over the charge of keeping Utopia in shape.

The slave cyborgs were the first to fall. They wrangled with their owners, snatched their electrocuting sticks, and cut themselves free. Loose on the Utopian streets and euphoric at their newfound freedom, they bumped into the cockroaches. Some cyborgs were seen roaming around with flashes of sparks over their heads. Their robot parts were crashing. While others, whose robot sides took over, incessantly carried on a single task repeatedly. Over 65% configuration cyborgs were found building bridges, dismantling them, and delivering the same parcels to different places, occasionally to the cockroaches. They weren't programmed to rest.

In the absence of US-Δs, ψs sent random help calls in space. Not knowing how to reach Saros, they constantly raised alarms shooting out to far corners. The Rhinos of Lucas looked up and saw wanton shooting stars in the sky. They geared up for another round of kicks.

If there was a trace of sanity left, it was in the Σs, who were working round the clock in a futile attempt to restore order. More than a dozen mars moons had passed since they had switched themselves off to cool their systems. And now overheated and overworked, they too had occasional sparks over their heads. They sped and retarded their work unwillingly and were ever so more irritable. They began biting their roach captivators.

The robot masters, without their cyborgs, went askew, too, as they hadn't been fed any other task. They now sprawled idle in the corners or sometimes even on the mid-streets. Some even switched themselves off and lay splayed to rust.

But roaches had to do what they had to do.

Dracko hovered over the lot of them arresting his roads. "Yo Scavy, it fails to my reason that you forsook your live breathing form to become a tin can, but you still kept your grisly six limbs. With all that power, shouldn't you have thought about a better look or perhaps even a better brain?"

The roaches were unmoved.

"But of course, you needed a brain for it. Hmm. Catch-22. You need a brain to ask for a brain. Cold-blooded creeps. Just as I thought."

Dracko's patience was waning. He flipped to his humanlike habit of humming his favorite tune. Usually, his quirks went unnoticed, yet another noise in a world of noises. But this time something unexpected happened. The roaches couldn't absorb the sound like the cyborgs. They skidded, toppling over one another. Dracko paused, and lifted his brow. The roaches were stable again. He resumed his humming, albeit louder this time, and they poured like a rainshower from their high perches. His smirk grew, and he readjusted the volume, tempo, and pitch to measure the effect. With every rising note and decibel, the roaches got more disheveled.

Dracko floated to the G-4's oversight tower. It was a sorry sight with all the mayhem left by the cockroaches. Without any US-Δ to stop him, he sneaked effortlessly into the bulletin room and carefully eyed the forty-three volume controls. Using his thought-effecting device, he slid them all to the maximum.

Seconds later, a deafening voice boomed in Utopia. "Hello. Hello. Roachies. May I have your attention, please? Your very own Dracko is speaking. Your host for the evening."

The still roach blanket covering Utopia began to waver .Dracko continued: "That makes me wonder we have nothing but evenings here. Hmm."

"Too bad," Dracko yelled, shaking the structures at the far end.

The cockroaches scampered for shelter, scuttling under one another.

"Yeah. That's the spirit, roachies. I admire your zest. Here let me entertain you. Sing a song to celebrate your arrival."

Dracko's voice shook the Utopian skies as he sang Frank Sinatra's song.

"Dai dut the denny in a dum-dot, dai dut the denny in a dum-dot

Do det the daper and dai det the dum, cause dai dut the denny in the dum-dot.

[What's you say?]

I put the penny in the gum-slot, I put the penny in the gum-slot,

You get the paper and I get the gum, 'cause I put the penny in the gum-slot.

[Eeny meeny minee mo, turn the handle, let it go,]

[Peppermint flavor yummy yum, I got the penny and I get the gum,]

['Cause dai dut the denny in the dum-dot,] I put the penny in the gum-slot.

Do det the daper and dai det the dum

Cause dai dut the denny in the dum-dot."

His words shook the nearby structures toppling the Σs alongwith the cockroaches. The former cursed and bit their fellow fallers mid-flight, while the latter dropped like feathers only to find themselves scuttling fast and contesting one another for space in narrow slits.

They fled in droves clearing up spaces for the Utopian skies. Vespa received thousands of distressed calls. The first few responders bounced off Utopia's periphery, courtesy of Dracko's anthem.

But if anything, the roaches had always been the masters of modifications. They infiltrated Utopia wearing shock absorbers with an immediate mission to arrest Dracko.

They planted and detonated massive energy bombs under the bulletin room, exploding the head of G-4's surveillance tower where Dracko was operating. The sound system crashed, and once again Utopia was buried under the flitting cockroaches' deep blackness and unsettling hum.

With the sun, Utopia's only source of light, cut by the cockroaches, the temperature plunged. Σs had a harder time monitoring the dark alleys. Everything that could go loose was out on the utopian streets now. Smoke rose from crashing robots. Fires arose in clumps. And astray cyborgs climbed up the dilapidated G-4's tower along with the cockroaches.

Far away in the space, different disappointments were arraying up for Vespa. In Lucas, the cockroaches had traced back their stomped and crashed sensors but found no trace of the Soul machine. The discovery turned a case of intrigue into an emergency, for a full human on the loose was dangerous.

A dark cloud of cockroaches was gathering over Bella-Dilla. Its deafening buzz woke the slumbering stars up, who were equally disappointed with Vespa's inept handling of the human and the live roach. Added to it was the distaste of having roaches around them.

An urgent deliberation was declared, and the old star spoke.

"Honorable members, we have a situation here. What we always feared, the despicable roaches have brewed trouble again for the Universe. And our sources signal that one among them, a live roach, is out loose with a full human now. The Star community has always appreciated the inquisitiveness of our human companions, but we are also well aware of the whammy their adventure has brought forth. I call upon your attention and insight to contain this impending hazard."

Their wise whispers quickly drowned in the cacophony of the witches, who watched the overcast from the peripheries of their blue fog.

"Oh. My. My. It looks like there's some strong hatred brewing in there", said the Queen. The seventy sisters huddled around her.

"What do you think it could be?" she asked Zu.

The mongoose pressed his glasses up and squirmed up his nose. "As ludicrous as it may sound, that blot appears like the nasty cockroaches, but of course, at a distance like this, my opinion is precarious, My lady."

The loathly laughter of the cannibals, now beaten to a defeated whine, breezed in weakened rebuttal. And the husky voice said: "Told ya. Marrisa is astray. Marissa will pay."

The cloud quickly grew into a mighty storm. First for its kind, in its expanse and urgency, it chickened out the stars and the witches alike. The Queen looked askew over at her sisters, whose shine was fading, hiding behind one another.

Their mongooses, too, cowered behind them.

"Pftt," she whistled to Zu and flew at an ear's distance from the group. Zu leapt after her.

"What do you think it is?"

"Despicable cockroaches of Vespa, my lady, indisputable now."

"Why here?"

"Can't say? An infraction."

She looked again at the growing cloud. This time blinking strong: "Doesn't appear to be one. Can we take them over with our shine?"

Zu readjusted his glasses and calculated on his fingertips for a long time, pausing and recounting again. By the time he declared: "two million and twenty-two, odds aren't in our favor," the cockroach cloud was blanketing the horizon.

Marissa had to fall back this time.

"Ladies," she said and clapped for attention. "May I have your attention, ladies? As you can see, the hatred of the universe is trying to take over Bella-Dilla. It's the moment we feared. But history bears witness that we had always defended our love shine no matter what." She passed a sideway stare to the cannibals and darted to the sisters. "Onward to Pleritus. Wild witches can follow if they please." And as if the sisters had been waiting, they flew even before her.

Devoid of any option, the cannibals followed, whimpering and sulking. Tailing, the group hopped wicked Bizzy, creating sobbing sounds. "Bizzy had her love juice stolen by Marissa. Marrisa must pay."

At a sufficient distance from the cloud, now that Marissa could think, she said to Zu, "I knew that one was a bad omen with all that dirt and darkness shrouding her." Her eyes were shrunk with suspicion. "She doesn't know much about us anyway." She blinked a few times and then stared at Zu . "Or does she?"

Zu's heart froze. He leapt a few steps and stole his glance, squirming away from her, "Nary, my Beloved Queen. Not in the seventh universe."

"And so I thought. Bella-Dilla had always kept itself away from the muck of the universe, and so shall we in the future."

In his head, Zu replayed his conversation with Wu-C2 and hoped it would remain a secret.

Chapter 7: Sand-land Pleritus

The masters of memory and gatekeepers of all records that had existed right from the ice age to the governance of the Saros, the oldest living beings, the Pleritus trees knew the sins of all and were aggrieved with their knowledge. Deep and wide as their roots were, they entwined intricately with one another and passed on the information they gathered during their lifetime. Their fibers were filters stacking the most important information in readily accessible layers.

For centuries, many of them had desired to settle their dues with humans to narrate the damage the humans had caused. At the root of this longing was their desire to be considered the wisest in the Universe. And a chastisement sermon to humans was their perfect chance. But with humans' disappearance, this desire had parked in the backdrop too.

Unlike their animal kins, they spoke in rustles.

"What's that?" one commented on the Soul machine perched atop a big bog. Unaware of the growing rustles and astonished by a floating sea of greys and greens in a world of indistinct shades and shadows, Wu-C2 tried to focus harder. A forest, albeit an unusually quiet one.

Giant spiky trees thrummed to the winds and reached tall for the sky. Wu-C2 hoisted herself on the dashboard and looked up from the spreading skylight. A chilly gust of wind brushed her hair, sending a bolt of shivers down her spine and thrusting a strong, musty smell up her nose.

The canopy spread far and wide, extending across ends. No trace of the sky anywhere. "A forest, Dodo," she said. Her voice echoed, "a forest, Dodo…Forest, Dodo."

A steady sprinkle brushed the scene ever so often. Wu-C2 waited for it to stop, and drops' constant drumming lulled her to a nap.

The Soul Machine was parked in the clearest patch of Pleritus, easily discoverable. It was a scare for Moon, who was stung by Wu-C2's ignorance. He lamented not telling her about the cockroaches and the G-4, their aversion to intergalactic travel, and the threat they possessed. But considering the need of the moment, sending unnecessary frequencies would have been a somewhat perilous option, so he sulked and cussed but waited.

"Get off that goddamn patch, Woozy Do."

The evening spread its cloak, a reawakened bird readying for a long flight rendering the patchy grey ground with various shades of black. Something seemed different. Wu-C2 sat upright. The wind. She listened. It was blowing in patterns and rustled ever so slowly. Wu-C2 turned her translator on.

The trees were talking. "What's that? Never seen that before."

"I know what it is. It is a human."

They were swaying now, creaking and leaning over the Soul Machine. Their tall crowns touched it, blocking the sporadic streaks of sunshine that it was receiving somehow.

"Ain't no humans put up here. We banished your kind. Go away."

Whispers. Groans. Mutters.

To make things worse, the drizzle turned into heavy showers, and Wu-C2 couldn't hear a thing. Just the heavy plop of falling droplets the size of boulders that could have made a dent if they hit her head.

The Soul Machine was now half submerged in water.

Moon leaned over his screen. "For God's sake, get out of there, Woozy Do. It's Pleritus; the rains never cease. And those trees can talk you to death."

Emptied of their weensy pools of energies, the trees were standing upright again. In their eagerness to wait for a human, they had missed the operational aspect of it: how would they speak so many words? With abundant and unobstructed streams of light, Wu-C2 could see now.

She decided to step out and hoisted herself up the Soul machine's skylight. A thunderous slap hit her hard. That which appeared to be a strong wind inside the machine was a deafening and raging storm outside. It was thick, choking her eyes, making it hard for her to see.

Wu-C2 closed her eyes and exerted ahead. Plop! She squelched on the mulch.

Moon hissed: "Why Woozy Do? Of all the places she could land in the safest Pleritus, she chooses the most unsafe muck. And if that's not it, she has this crazy idea of leaving the machine behind."

Dracko's voice breezed in: "A quintessential human trait."

"Hologram. You broke loose from the cockroaches?"

Dracko raised his eyes, and his famous smirk swept his face.

"Moon, my friend. I always thought the human in you was smarter. Are you forgetting that being the hologram I am, I can simultaneously be at many places? Those goddamn cockroaches are busy thinking what to do of me. For now, they have the most bizarre notion of having me captured. Let them have their joy." His smirk grew ever so more.

Moon gave a slight nod of appreciation and pointed to the screen. "Tell me how come her sensors aren't raising the alarm."

This time Dracko, too, had no answers. He studied the screen silently. Wu-C2 is clumsily wading through the muck. "Interesting. Never seen a cyborg behave like that before."

With every next step Wu-C2 took, she was leaving the Soul Machine and Dodo farther behind her. The mush was getting softer and she exerted more to pull her leg out. With that extra force, she sank further. The more she exerted, the deeper she dropped and harder her march got.

The forest around her came alive. Apparently, the trees weren't appreciating the idea of losing the opportunity of haranguing the last human they caught hold of. It wasn't short of a miracle that one dropped from the heavens on her own in a million years. And they spoke in prolonged moans.

"Fifty thousand years ago, humans came on Earth."

Wu-C2 was neck deep in the muck trying to make sense of the endless drawls and rustles of the trees. But then she stopped for a moment and saw something she had been missing all this while, the big yellow eyes peering out from the darkness. She knew what this was. The tiny super-monkeys with a tail curled nine times, and two long pointed ears that worked as radars. Perched upside-down on the high branches, they could almost be called cute. But when they spread their enormous spiky wings, they expanded into giant nasty-looking creatures who flew with the speed of rockets, leaving a fire trail behind them and burning all they crossed to ashes." To the planet's relief, those occasions were rare. For now, piqued by the presence of these new guests, the monkeys huddled in the canopy.

"And that was the beginning of the end." The trees continued.

Many miles away, a graver danger was enfolding. The G-4, erect with one yellow unblinking eye askew on his head and his severed innards dangling out from severed side of his upright body, watched his bugs sink in the Pleritus bog. His army was now reduced to three-fourths. Unlike Wu-C2, the bugs were too impatient to stay still. There were no super monkeys to distract them, and there was another reason for their fast collapse:

In Pleritus, nothing harmed you as long as you meant no harm. But if you did, even the slightest bit, the planet used all its might to quarantine you. Swallow you deep in its infinite bog. Never to release you again.

G-4 decided to leave the sinking bugs to their fate and moved on. The remainder of his bugs scurried over the tree tops to get a better view of the surroundings. And sure, they found unusual commotion of the monkeys at the distant end where Wu-C2 was immobilized.

G-4 grabbed the trees with his thick limbs and hoisted himself up from the ground. He latched himself to the high branches with extendable robot arm and reinforced the grip with his strong titanium leg. Taking long leaps from one tree to another, he briskly darted toward Wu-C2. While doing so, he left a backdrop of destruction, slashing and burning all he was leaving behind.

Wu-C2, unaware of the impending danger and Moon's

annoyance, was intrigued by her strange society: the trees and monkeys.

"Humans, they destroyed all."

Wu-C2 mused: "Bees. They must be around if super monkeys are. And the wish frogs too." The wish frogs, rare as they were thought to be, weren't that rare, but they had this uncanny ability to blend into the backgrounds or change their appearance into someone you loved. The only way to locate them was their distinct and loud sound, "Tarr." A slight relief, nevertheless an obstruction. Its nuisance was unacceptable to the slumbering trees who moaned and bickered, so the frogs mostly kept to themselves and produced the sound ever so low that only the most fortunate could hear them.

Meanwhile, the trees carried on with their discourse. "They made fires, and they burned many of us alive." The rustles were getting sharper.

Water trapped in Woozy's splattered hair was obstructing her view, dripping one drop at a time, tracing the profile of her chiseled face, pooling up in her eyes and blurring her view. With her mouth still free, she could have caught the branches, but the miffed trees sulked and retracted and stood taller than ever.

"Ain't no humans put up here. Go away. This is not your place. Your kind has always been devious."

The swell was almost kissing the tip of Wu-C2's mouth and constricted her from all ends. She pressed her lips together to prevent it from leaking into her mouth and could march no more. The night tightened its grip, and the trees sunk in slumber, their erect defenses clumsily shriveled now, giving a clear open-wide view of the sky; A Kaleidoscope of stars, moons, and galaxies.

Trees continued their bickering in their sleep. "They cut us to make hideous papers that they dropped in the waste basket. They printed garish claptrap on us."

Their haranguing didn't bother the monkeys much, who wrapped their tails and hung upside down beneath each other, snoring and occasionally flapping their wings at the slightest sounds and turning their head with short head tilts and "tut-tuts."

Out in the distance, the trail of fires was inching closer, illuminating the skies. From the corners of her eyes, Wu-C2 could see the silhouette spreading in the far end. She dozed off, wondering what that could be.

Back on Earth, Moon was increasingly getting baffled by Wu-C2's behavior. Even sending frequencies wouldn't have helped now. There was no way the Soul Machine could have pulled Wu-C2 out from that insidious muck.

Wu-C2 woke up to a cacophony of the investigator bees. With their golden antennas like twigs on fire and their blood-red color, those bees made the daybreak scene a tango of flames. They nudged the trees for information and recorded everything in their antennas. "No source untouched" was their motto.For a moment, they pondered upon the possibility of securing information from Wu-C2. But with a single look at her clenched mouth and they dropped their pursuit to move on.

By now the smidgen of the night grew into a thick black and red smoke pier that surged up to the skies, inching closer every moment. The darkle engulfed all in sight and became too overwhelming to evade. About time, the bees and monkeys veered to it, leaving an unusual calm and stillness behind.

The drizzle got intense, alerting the world about the impending disaster. A high drama of light and shadows continued above with the trees towering back into the skies. Wu-C2 wasn't sinking anymore, held in place by the ground underneath her that was hardening.

"Tarr. Tarr.

"Thinking of me? Ho ho ho." She looked up to find Moon's wish-frog hanging upside down from the giant tree in front of her.

Moon's wish-frog took the clue from her bewildered eyes: "Oh yes. I can. This and many other things." With his head populated with thick spiky hair and his shoulders stouter, he looked a younger version of Moon. He winked and folded his hands on his chest, and swung.

Restrained all over, Wu-C2 squeezed her eyes hard. The mud around her had stiffened, and G-4's destruction had painted everything in different tinges of red. Wu-C2 looked up at the trees stretching themselves to see the source of the blaze.

But Moon wish-frog was unfazed by the drama. He smiled beatifically, and his eyes glittered. "That mud, a dangerous one, my dear. Swallows anything that wades into it. Tarr Tarr."

The trees snapped and rustled: "Quit your tattle."

Moon wish-frog swung once and rustled in the manner of trees: "My apologies."

Ancient trees stood erect again, and he resumed his

chatter: "I see you have quite a few wishes. Hmm. To reunite the world? That's quite an unusual one. Now, why would you want to do that, Woozy Do?"

Wu-C2 muttered some incomprehensible words from her restrained mouth.

He worded her thoughts. "Because they are all bored to death. Now, that's an interesting viewpoint."

This made the trees curious, and instead of reprimanding the wish frog, they leaned to hear him translate Wu-C2's thoughts.

Wish-frog nodded and reiterated, "As I was saying, that's an interesting thought. Why do you think they are bored? Isn't this a peaceful world now?"

Wu-C2 took a while to think this through.

"I..I...They have no use of their life."

The trees, who too had been greatly lamenting their lost role in the universe, rustled vigorously appreciating Wu-C2's understanding.

"You've got the audience, Woozy Do. As noble as the task may seem, I am afraid it is beyond my capabilities. Do you have another wish, Woozy Do?"

"I see you wish to be free. Interesting," he swung back and forth.

Moon wish-frog eyed the growing blaze: "And considering the trouble you are in, it's a wise wish."

He whistled twice.

Heavy thrums grew near and far. A monstrous dark shadow loomed on the horizon, on the opposite end of the smoky turf. But unlike the slow-paced thickening pier, it darted fast and parked itself over Wu-C2: a fuzzy cloud resembling the shape of a giant fish.

Pleased with his agility and rejoicing the moment with a smug, Moon wish-frog swung on the branch. "Ho ho ho. Presenting the king wish whale. Mightiest of all. Catch its fins and hop on before it disappears again. Tarr Tarr."

The cloud descended on Wu-C2, and she latched on to its dangling fin with her mouth, her teeth digging in the soft fluff. It seemed surprisingly solid for its shadowy front. Soon as Wu-C2 secured her grip, it began to float away, pulling her out, and she could hold the fin with both hands. With a single swing of her hand, Wu-C2 hoisted herself on the solid carpet-like base. Perched atop a desert of cotton white sand, she saw tiny creatures scuttling just about everywhere. The tired old fishes traveled on crab backs, and the octopuses took shifts to bridge the gaps in the crevices and bulges.

"Hello there," said Wu-C2 to a couple of pouting blood-red fishes riding an equally red crab.

Outraged at this abrupt disturbance, the crab retreated and jumped up to claw at Wu-C2's nose bringing the fishes perched over right at Wu-C2's eye level. They said in their puffy voices: "We don't waste time in waste words like hullo. Come quick and ask what work needs to be done. Ain't no Hullo again. Quick, for we have no time to waste for waste words like Hullo. We are the corporate trout." They said together, flapping their fins.

"But. ..I...I don't have any work. I...I just wanted to say well," she corrected her throat: "say Hello."

Wu-C2's words brought the cloud to a standstill, and they gasped: "What? No work? Impossible. How did that happen? It's a scandal." They cried together.

A dozen crabs scuttled to surround Wu-C2 and various fishes jumped over them. The red fishes forced a tiny needle thermometer between Wu-C2's lips; others held a micro stethoscope against her chest. A dozen others clung to her hair, stretching a damp cloth on her head. One scaled fish pressed its ears on Wu-C2's wrist and searched for her heartbeat. She raised her fin to say:

"The heartbeat is ok."

"Temperature is fine."

"Brain is ok too."

Together they cried, "Then what is wrong? No work. Something's wrong. So wrong."

"Check again," One panic-struck panting fish announced with her fins flitting hard. "Find it. Work is waiting."

This time many more fishes, big and small, put their ears on Wu-C2 —here and there, everywhere. Those who could not put their ears directly on her latched theirs on the next fish.

"Nerves ok. Muscles ok. Liver ok. Lungs ok." Together they cried, "Then what is wrong?"

A fleet of thoughtful red fishes darted to and fro, muttering, "What is wrong? What is wrong?"

Anxious crabs put their claws to dispirited rest, and octopuses weren't bridging the gaps anymore. A deep melancholy took over the sandland.

One gloomy-looking fish with the most extended face and a protruding belly came forward and said in a grave voice, "My dear fishes. We have a situation. It looks like those nasty whispering trees are up to a nuisance again. They are jobless, and they don't want anyone to work. They don't have any goals." He slid to Wu-C2's side, maintaining his composure, and tucked at his fin twice to straighten it. "This here is their first messenger. A virus. And it is a failure on the guardian monkeys' and investigator bee's part to let the virus spread."

Groans and gasps grew. Fishes and crabs were repulsed, and the red couple released Wu-C2's nose to drop flat on the ground.

"If the virus spreads and we stop working. What will happen to the sandland? To Pleritus? Who will keep it going?" one fish cried.

"What will happen? What will happen?" they repeated.

The sulky-looking fish captured the occasion to speak: "A life without work is a damned life. About time we confront those trees."

"Yes. All they do is stand there and say dragging nasty waste words eating up our precious time." Someone spoke out aloud.

Those words made the old fish uncomfortable: "Though in speaking that we are wasting some more time." He looked anxiously at his watch and pointed at the sand land clock. An extensive "OH" followed as the octopus serving as the arms of the clock was deep into the conversation, and the clock too had stopped working.

In that moment of fury, the fishes began pushing Wu-C2 to the edge of the whale and back into the muck. "Rid of the virus."

From the edge, Wu-C2 could see the dark smoke-tornado, the familiar bugs whirling in it. It made her heart jump. Then she saw Moon wish-frog still dangling from the tree. "You've got to help me, Moon." She yelled.

"Umm. Let me see. Tarr. Tarr." He began counting on his fingers, rubbed his eyes, and counted again.

"Stop that nuisance." The trees cried.

Wu-C2 was almost on edge. "Be quick."

Moon wish-frog counted and recounted.

"What are you counting?"

"You have 10 minutes. Now 9 minutes and 50 seconds to make your last wish." He said aloud.

"What wish?" cried WU-C2. Her words came out loud as thunder stunning the scuttling creatures.

The fishes scrambled to the edge. They gawked. One cried out aloud: "There it is. A wish, frog! There. Dangling from that tree."

Chaos ensued. All that was on that cloud yearned to lay its hand on it.

The fishes began diving in clusters, topping on the muck and drowning one another. The crabs who were a bit smarter caught one another's legs and formed a dangling chain. Guardian monkeys didn't appreciate the drama and spread their wings and flew away, and trees began their moaning. "Just what we feared. A human means trouble."

Moon wish-frog smiled blandly: "Well. That makes it 2. Quick, your last wish, Wu-C2."

"I. I. Planet Earth. I want to reach the planet earth."

All was dark and still again.

Chapter 8: A change of plans

"That was close," Moon said, staring at the screen. The human heart in him was throbbing, and he smiled at the feel. He sank in his chair to let the wave rush to his brain, to flood his being. The chair reciprocated, turning soft and plush. The steadiness of earth's gravity accentuated its feel. They were buried in this fifteen-by-twenty-foot cocoon, many miles below the ground. The chair, him, and his chamber of creepy crawlies. That's all he brought with him. That was all he needed. And how marvelously the chair had worked it out. Shrouded in awe of this 4-legged's intelligence, he felt pleased and comfortable.

On the screen in front of him, the G-4 was still hovering over Pleritus, his decimated troops digging the muck, scooping the dropping crabs mid-air, and clinging on to the fading edges of the wish whale. The invasion was harder with diving fishes and crabs who took anything in their way, slinging down straight into the muck. Moon was delighted by this incredulous sight of the mightiest creatures befuddled by the innocuous workaholic crabs and fishes.

The unusual commotion in Pleritus had attracted the Vespian cockroaches' attention, who were now abandoning their search in Utopia and darting to Pleritus in droves. Moon gobbled up the sight and switched his view to Utopia. The fringes of tree houses were now visible through the deserted patches.

"This would take quite some time to settle. Ho. Ho. Ho." He said and swiped to the next screen.

The other half of G-4 had landed in the coldest corner

of Earth. Perched on the highest ridge, it supervised its robots, now scooping bucketfuls of ice everywhere. Moon had an inkling of why G-4 had chosen this spot. This was the only easy-to-inquire lot left. The rest was tricky with its mines, chemicals, and toxic trash. Underground had not yet occurred to the G-4. Moon wasn't sure for how long.

Now that he had some time, he mulled at the spontaneity of it all and where it had landed him and Woozy. How she had seen what he did not intend her to see. And how miraculously she had survived the crashes. Even Vespa. Did he underestimate her? Could she be the next whole human? He had an intense urge to laugh but was robbed of the moment by a massive thud followed by a couple of deep groans. The ground shook, disorienting everything.

On the shaking screen in front of him, Moon watched the volcano puking tons of hot stuff and gases . He stared in awe at the vivid colors flying all over. Even the sea flaunted the blood-red sprinkles before swallowing them up and sinking them back to their source.

Woozy. He had to do something about her before roaches and G-4 cleared the chaos between them. As for him, the chair, and the chamber, they seemed to be safe, for now. The surface was so hot that any metal brute, no matter how formidable, was likely to get reduced to ashes. Those critters were going to take their sweet time tracing their way down to him. But Woozy was out in the open.

Moon stood in front of the universe map again. With Pleritus out, and the Bella-Dilla witches rejecting Woozy, his options were close to nil. Then he thought of something unusual and even unlawful. Could he send Wu-C2 back in time? Dangerous as it was, Saros had banned it at the beginning of the Universe. Moon needed a second vote and thought of the only one he had always reached out to, Dracko.

Back in Utopia, Dracko hovered under a spotlight, his long face wavering in ebbs and troughs. His frown creating a deep ridge between his eyebrows, but his smirk still intact. "Well. Well. I can hear you twinkies rumbling around. I hear you still buried in chambers out there. Huh? Not the sharpest way for the most powerful planet."

In the shadows next to the spotlight, hundreds of cockroaches skittered. While they had frozen the metal parts of the batty cyborgs, they had little clue how to deactivate this hologram that was speaking incessantly. His booming voice that shook the chamber hurt their movements, making them skid off the steel walls. Dracko's volume grew, and a few critters slid out to the chamber's entryway to escape it. His roads floated idly on top of one another.

"Been fifteen mars moon, and you've not found a speck. Come to the reason of it, could it be that you are looking at the wrong place or that there's nothing to find or for that matter, to look?"

The cockroaches scurried about indifferently. Dracko resumed his humming at a greater volume tumbling them from their perches.

Soon as he was off-focus, his facsimile appeared in front of Moon.

"Hmm," he said, pondering the difficult question in front of them. "Why am I not surprised? Those goddamn witches always mishmash things."

"Not just them. There's something odd about it all. Cannibals going after her and then her acting on her instincts in the bog. That's not how she had been programmed. Her controls had shut down on their own."

"Um Hmm," Dracko pondered.

"Has she somehow transformed into a full human? Have we missed something?"

"Interesting" Drcako raised his brow, " depends on your spans of inattentiveness. It makes me question, did you doze off?" He danced his brows.

Moon stole his eyes away from Dracko.

"The roach. It seems alive too. Who in this universe would be interested in reviving a roach except you?"

A heavy silence descended on them.

"As unlikely as it seems, there is only one explanation. Somehow the cockroaches got wind of our travelers and turned our cyborg into a full-blown human."

Dracko considered the possibilities. A prominent one was of losing Wu-C2 to G-4 or the roaches.

"How much time you took to create her."

"Almost a century."

"Say you send her on time travel."

"She will be out of reach then. We may not get her back."

"Do we have a choice?"

"Not really."

Moon had to say what he had to say "What if we let her become a full human? Now that she already is in her physical form."

Moon once again took a good look at the bug-shrouded Utopia. As he watched the cockroaches inspect the wish whale and skitter to G-4, he retraced the path of the Soul

Machine. This time not on the X and Y axis of the space but on the Z axis of depth and time.

"Soul Travel?" he said. "We link Woozy's experiences to the humans she visits."

"That's audacious, given what happened to Haruto."

Soul Travel wasn't a new phenomenon. In the 2050s, humans discovered that the universe wasn't constant progress in time and space. Instead, it was a dimensionless realm experiencing and improving itself continuously from millions of angles simultaneously. It worked in layers, constantly learning and re-implementing its behaviors to learn even more in the next layer. At any point, if a human's senses could be connected to the perception of another human, the connecting human could travel back in time.

But there was a glitch — while doing so, the receiving human forgot her original form and became the other human in entirety. That is how she learned.

"That, my friend, is the most bizarre plan I have heard. And regressive." Dracko said, reminiscing the last time he had known of it.

Moon traced another line from Pleritus to Earth.

"And here's our disguise."

While Wu-C2 will travel in time, Dodo will travel in space to Utopia to lure away the G-4 and the roaches.

And sure, it worked. Soon as Dodo darted out, the monitors veered to the Soul Machine, and Wu-C2 sneaked out unnoticed. Moon stole the opportunity to connect with Wu-C2.

"Listen up, Woozy Do. You will be traveling in time now. You can go to the future or the past, be anyone you want.

And you can choose to stay back. Now, tell me, Woozy Do, who would you want to be? What would you like to know?"

A long static broke his voice.

"The end. I want to go to the end of the earth."

"That's a fantastic choice, Wu-C2. The end is the best place to reroll." Said Dracko.

Before Dodo could hit the Utopian borders, the machine was captured by cockroaches.

Chapter 9: Haruto Amuro

"Take me to the humans of 2043, and find Haruto Amuro." Moon said.

Many thousands of hazy lights began flickering around. A few bounced off.

An orb grew in size, and the rest receded in the background.

"Coordinates, please."

Moon copied the data from Haruto Amuro, dragged and pasted it in Wu-C2's window. Next, he deactivated Wu-C2's file.

The thing about time travel was that it buried you deep in history. You became unreachable. No matter how evolved, any outsider couldn't find you even when they knew you were somewhere between the endless layers of eternity. With Wu-C2 traveling on the Z axis of time now, not even Moon could reach her. But, one thing was certain no cockroaches or G could track her here. Not until she chose to come back. Choice was the biggest power a human had.

Wu-C2 was shapeless like some cotton cloud, like ether without anything solid to hold her. The great disappointment greeted her yet again. A familiar landscape: masked people, lanes, mars dust, and plain towering buildings housing thousands of bunkers; all gray, bland and flat. Was Earth a copy of Utopia?

She floated aimlessly for a while, scanning the surroundings. Where were those mystical earthly things Moon talked about?

The boredom led her to a tall black man flanked by two

white guards. His walk was the weirdest. With a stooped back, he walked, dragging his feet mechanically as if hauling a load beyond his capabilities. He put one step forward and waited several seconds to put another. The guards walking with him almost seemed peeved by this lethargy. In the world of conformity, even a single act of clumsy non-conformance looked like a rebellion. They passed many stations and tree habitats for what seemed like an eternity, finally halting in front of a sealed metal chamber. Wu-C2 knew this place. She sighed. A cabin.

This was where they replaced masks and aging body parts and gave immunity shots. Wu-C2 wondered how many immunity shots they had here. In Utopia, the count ran to five, at max seven. Those big jabs were ghastly. The thought made Wu-C2 shudder.

She looked at the wheatish man again, and an odd feeling rose her spine — sympathy? She readily relinquished the thought of going inside. Those invisible layers of lasers could burn an intruder to ashes even before she became aware of the contact. Wu-C2 had to wait outside.

Time moved slower than a snail. She dwelled on her human side, wondering what Moon must be doing. With him, time was easy. Especially when he told her stories of different lands where he bumped into non-human creatures, she wondered about the dangers in those stories. In particular, one big giant teethy creature that ripped humans and cyborgs apart, bit by bit. Leaving them strewn out in a massive space for their parts to pick themselves up painstakingly. Woozy's imagination gave it forms, sometimes of a fiery giant robot, other times of a G-4 with big red eyes.

The red blinker on top of the gates was flashing now.

Wu-C2 straightened. They will be out any moment. But Wu-C2's caution was undue. It was just the slouching man. He had been released.

She followed him, dragging himself in his awkward walk to his station, and veer to his bunker, where he dropped dead to sleep: his face buried in the hardened mattress, his masks, controls, and suit still on, a repugnant body odor indicating 100% human. He was snoring now. Before long, his contagious slumber leached into Wu-C2, and she too dozed off.

The sky was dim when she woke up. And though she was awake, she had a dreamlike feeling. She reached out and touched the mattress that felt coarse and stiff like a stick. Heaviness enveloped her, and a gloom that bled her body out of its vigor settled in her heart. She felt old and fragile. The enormous effort to sit up kicked up a slouch on her back, and she sat with her bony legs dangling from the edge of the bed. Wu-C2 looked wearily at them. Nothing like the smooth, well-formed, crafted to perfection, and sportive ones she had always known. But instead, an unappealing hard, dry, and famished version. Her breath that came in gusts was slow and laborious, a beaten-down effort to stick to yet another moment of life.

She stood up and plucked the badge by her bedside. The words were hazy to her eyes. She read them anyway: Haruto Amuro. Habits took over, and with a slap of her hand, she stuck it on her chest and clambered out of the bunk into the common corridor.

Wu-C2 was changing. With every step, she was more Haruto Amuro and less Wu-C2. Her memory was fading, and she sank deep into the despair so intimate to Amuro.

Wu-C2 soon was a forgotten dream.

A swarm of masked faces engulfed her. From up above, they looked like zigzagging dots in a two-dimensional field. But a trained eye could see that they bridged variations in their heights by wearing different leveled footwear.

A perfect picture of boredom and uniformity: dress, colors, height, weight, everything that can be seen from a naked human eye. Haruto sighed at the sorry sight. Years ago, he had caught a glimpse of his face when they were replacing his masks. How wonderful it looked. That pale skin with its tinges of red was electrifying. Were those masked faces the same as him or were they different? He wondered. Mask-free, he was so vulnerable. The sense was overwhelming in the big blue capsule, under completely sanitized conditions and pure air with 21% oxygen. He could almost touch and feel his warmth: the air, free and wild, flooding his lungs. His skin was soft and electrifying. And though every part in him wanted to do that again, once out, he felt safe under the mask again —familiar bondage. Maskless, he was awkward, skewed, and most naked, even to himself.

Haruto was now walking on a sparkling street. He paused occasionally and looked straight up at those tree habitats. They seemed to reach out to the sky in an effort to yank it down. He wanted to yank something too—those mighty habitats. An urge grew in him to climb up but the glare was blinding. He wanted to scoot up as fast as he could to that point where the trees kissed the grey sky. His eyes burned and welled up.

In reality, he was looking straight at those suits walking in six colors: red, blue, yellow, white, black, and grey. They walked in lanes, a thousand of them. From a bird's eye, they appeared like infinite patterns of colored lines. Donning the reds were bright young women, blue were young men, yellow were teens, and white were seasoned men and women. The diseased were subdued in grey. He didn't prefer to notice them much.

He was in a blue suit with a slate tag, and he was in the second last lane, the long lane of blues. A young man, working-class walking in the lane of his kind. But he didn't mind, for this was his chance to walk next to reds, young women. Sometimes he stole a whiff of fragrance floating aimlessly around them, one of those far and few things that still managed to escape the suits. It was an infraction, much to the delight of Haruto.

But this day was different. Today, the greys had stopped ahead of others blocking Haruto's reach to the reds. On this day, Haruto detested the greys even more. They could have been contagious. Who knew which new virus they carried? Getting rubbed now and then by them was atrocious. It was the obscenest invasion of his personal space. He hated this and that. But mostly, he hated them blocking his reach to the reds. An extreme bubble of disgust filled his heart. He watched the reds dissolve in the background behind the greys. That night, he fell into his bunker and sank deep into layers of black. In his dream, he ran through grey tunnels and found himself standing in front of a large grey wall. That fragrance, he sought it with his life, he knew it was around, but he couldn't quite catch it. Instead, a musty smell of the grays invaded his senses.

The nightmare followed him for days at a stretch. Haruto wanted to scream. It drove him mad. As such, life was very unthinkable, with everything marked and directed. It was standard and comfortable. Sometimes he had to think about which officer's instructions he had to follow while working. At such times, he immediately stood up and pinged his supervisor, Ted Neo. He had never seen Neo, but it wouldn't have mattered even if he had, for he had already seen too many red, blues, black, and whites. How different could he be? Could Neo have helped him with this predicament?

There was no Neo in his dream. The scream inside him grew louder and louder. Some nights, Haruto was jolted back to reality. When he sat beside another human, he wanted to tell them some things and hear some things in turn. Anything. He didn't know what he needed to speak and hear and how. So he just watched them with a lump in his throat while snacking on packs and packs of the nuts he carried. When he was done with them, he stomped on them with as much strength as he could muster. This indeed drew eyes towards him. Sets that quickly looked away.

Haruto was sitting in a trolley that took him to lane number 112. For 11 years, he never missed it. He reached exactly at 9:15 a.m., not a second early or late. It was a world of constants. The only inconstant were the days when the massive ball of fire in the sky rose a little and sank a little. Not much but enough for a trained eye. That particular day the sky was hardly visible through the thick gray smog. Years back, he saw a red patch there. Most memorable. He couldn't etch out the memory of the big mountain erupting on the street screens. A volcano. He had been yearning to see that again.

But the State had become vigilant and was now taking care of the emotion-riot the scene had caused. Now the sky looked painted blue in places. Especially so in the expanse of the volcano. But that wasn't it. Soon they were going to cover the glass doors and fixed windows with high-quality photographs of the morbid sky. A version of the sky that did not reflect any unwanted color or emotion.

The State made decisions for them. They said they were committed to stopping evil at its roots by plugging wrong thoughts. And because most thoughts were wrong, they decided to curb them altogether. But that was for the future. Currently, monitors and speakers at cross sections instructed people on right and wrong. And asked them to keep mum because words were inclined to become thoughts.

Their at-hand concern was to stretch the average life span. They had robots, but those weren't of much help, basically irritants. Among the impeccably dressed men, the robots were less perfect, for they shut themselves occasionally, or their parts had to be changed now and then. They demanded maintenance and were expensive, unlike men. They even became obsolete every 50 years or so. Keeping humans was easy. Unlike the robots, humans just needed a dozen immunity shots every month, and the work was done.

Perched on the sidewalk, Haruto watched the colors drift by. In the most unexpected event, a thought struck him. There was one hunched-back among them who wasn't anywhere now. The idea unleashed a chain of associations. Another walked with a limp. He was gone too. A couple more instances of memories, and he knew that suits moving into the diseased color never returned to gray. They looked weird: walking too close, once he even saw two of them grasping hands. "So close. Sick indeed."

The roadside screens beeped 8 Mars 220. He woke up like clockwork, boarded the 8:45 rail to work square, and slipped into his blue lane. The reds were walking right in the next lane. A whiff of sweet fragrance brushed his senses. This was a good day. From the corners of his eyes, he saw them drifting through the side lane. They walked with feather-light steps with a sway that brought flutters in his heart. One, in particular, was a strikingly different pair of blue eyes. Haruto was thunderstruck. He froze. The blue behind him bumped into him, thrusting him forward. Before he realized he felt his teeth digging into the flesh of his lips. The taste of blood was so different and so pleasant from the pills.

He hoisted himself up to see the set of those blue eyes fixed on him. His heart throbbed, ready to jump out of his suit.

Red was his color now. Her number was itched in his thoughts: 4278.

He watched her blend into the crowd. Those eyes chased away the grey walls of his dreams.

Soon he found himself peering into camouflaged eyes under translucent glasses: Blue, black, grey, round, sharp, and little. But they all were taken aback when he looked into them. Almost pleasantly violated. It was the beginning of an epidemic. Soon everybody was looking into everyone else's eyes. A glee infused the air. When they trudged in lanes, toiled at work, and tuckered in their bunkers, they were trying to find a certain set of eyes. They rubbernecked and nodded sheepishly.

Haruto knew all eyes, and they knew him too. They were turning bigger and brighter. A streak of mischief was growing in them. They fluttered and flitted. They looked up to him with anticipation as if asking him, "what's next."

The bubble in Haruto's heart grew. A fresh thought erupted in him to do something more, something better. He did not want to squash it. As he walked past the screens and the lanes, a certainty manifested in his gait, and a purpose flashed in his eyes. He could spot his red from a distance. The fidgety one with roving eyes. She was walking slowly, meeting all eyes that passed. Haruto heaved. He took more air than his lungs could handle, almost to the point of pain, and felt bloated for a moment. Twice his size. He closed his hands in a fist and darted straight to her, breaking the barrier in between. The lanes came to a standstill. Haruto looked into her eyes. A slight crinkle formed around them. He released his fist.

Alarms blared. "Abort. Back to lanes. Right now!"

The suits stayed to watch the spectacle.

The blood in Haruto's body was rushing fast, blocking every other sound. He took a few more steps toward her. Now they were standing face to face. He could smell her sweet perfume wafting ever so clearly. Haruto reached out for Red's hands. They fit like a glove in his.

The blue next to him did the same. Soon they were all holding hands.

The alarms blared louder this time. An army of black-dressed law-keepers surrounded the lanes. They were all separated by force.

Chaos ensued in the days that followed.

Utopia was quarantined. All smells and sounds were pulled away. Rogue deviants were thrust into quarantine camps and cabins. Facilities were flooded. Warnings blared on screens. Many suits were alarmed on their own and locked themselves up in their bunkers. A few rebellious ones ran free on the streets, their arms raised to the sky. They even stripped away their masks, their faces now distinct and naked to the world. The silent ones converged around Haruto and walked after him. They dismantled the dividers that made the lanes and ran holding hands out in the open.

Haruto felt his chest puff. This was his movement. There was something he had to do next. Out in the distance, the watch tower stood. He ran to it. The swarm followed him. Grabbing one rail at a time, he climbed up the great city clock and waved to the crowd. Euphoria grew. At the far end of the horizon, robots were mobilizing. He grabbed his mask and pulled it off, feeling the wind brush his cheeks and lift the chunks of his matted hair. His hands now felt moist. The suits below gasped at the sight.

Warning got louder. Haruto could hear them even from the top. "You are sick. Get back to your lanes now."

The crowd below looked at Haruto eager-eyed, waiting for another action. They walked together. What next? There had to be something next. They wondered. But Haruto had no clue. The robots were visible and under earshot now. Their hum was growing every moment. One blue suit released the hand he was holding. He slowly stepped away from the crowd and scampered to the lane leading to his bunker. Other eyes followed him.

Haruto could now see the G-2 perched up at the far facility tower. A swarm of robots circumventing him. The Suits saw him too and were now slipping back to the bunkers in rows. Their steps were heavier and sloppier than ever. At sunset, Haruto was the only one standing. His face was red and glowing in the evening sun. The tinker in his eyes was brighter under the pool of tears.

By now, the screens had converged around him. They spoke in unison. "You are sick. Get back to your lane. This is your last chance!" Haruto sank to his feet. He sat for a long time, watching the sun disappear. That night he was taken to the quarantine center and was drowned in a white light restrained inside a steel capsule. As Haruto's breath left his body, Wu-C2 regained her memories. She watched the fading city beneath her. There were no holding hands or mask-free faces. Like no Haruto ever lived. But one thing had changed. Robots moved in the centermost privilege lane. Their status was elevated, and they were considered more damage-proof than humans.

Something struck her. That face in the mirror. The face she saw down there. Moon was Haruto in his younger years.

He had always been a rebel.

Chapter 10: Death of G3 and The Birth of Moon

The lights were blinding, and Wu-C2 woke up with a shudder. A jolt of ice-cold sensation hit her, and she found herself confined in a frozen glass capsule inside a massive steel chamber. Her bare hands and legs were skinned to the pink layer underneath. Diametrically opposite to those of Haruto, they were hulky and crafted to precision, almost steel-like, however stout, like a stump. She was half the size of Haruto now.

Wu-C2 decided to step out. Naked and spooked, she downed her broad and webbed legs on the cold steel floor. Her short frame made the descent from her average size platform feel like a steep fall. Her face contorted along with her temperament. Things around looked minimalistic, but she detested them anyway. Hatred seeped into her heart. From this end to that end, giant screens surrounded her, data flipping through them in thousands per second. A single look at it, and she underscored the trend in it that was flat.

Aside from her capsule, the modest contents of her chamber included a side desk that flipped open from the steel wall and a suit — A G's suit. "G-. The third General of Justice city". She huffed. This was the last thing that she ever wanted to be.

Wu-C2 didn't don the G-suit, not yet. The traces of Woozy's psyche still sputtered in her new form, and she struggled to free herself from this gross, almost undeveloped body-mind. She tottered to the end and stood in front of a mirror visible in pockets between screens. The reflection in the mirror was horrendous: the face a ghastly art of gashes, and grey eyes piercing daggers. A flame of hatred burning bright in them, a standoff between absolute control and the fear of losing it.

Wu-C2's dainty spirit didn't take long to fizzle out and gave way to the heaviness and solidity of the G-3 settle: thick, imposing and strong. She was him now.

It was pointless seeing the face he had seen so many times; he huffed at the waste. His eyes sideswiped to the screen that said: "New virus, street 46."

Wasting no time, he stood up and put on his suit. He now stood towered over by a dozen armed humanoids with a Justice stamp traversing across their chests. One look, and he was repelled at his decision of placing them as the heads of their human troops. What exactly was he thinking? Justice City was far from perfect, and the paucity could be attributed to them. Their sole job was to make it perfect, but the place was far from it. An urge grew in him to trample them over, stomp at them with his heels. But an accompanying pinch of dread kept him from losing control. Two reasons: One, of course, his size was a third of those humanoids, and two, he questioned himself: "What if they had learned to reason, somehow on their own?" He pressed his lips tight, teeth grinding against one another, and said with an effort: "A rebel had been caught. The last was 163 years back." His breath was coming in heavy gusts.

Unaffected, the humanoids stood still and made their way as he stomped through the high and long corridors. He felt freezing iron in his spine, metal in his veins, and bubbling loathing in his heart. What a waste! His eyes noted everything that moved and didn't and kept a note of it. He remembered how he did it, singlehandedly muffled those inadequacies. And now this bunch of incompetent idiots was squandering everything he had built. But in his heart, he also knew it was different this time. Rebels had become more damaging and contagious. They were capable of multiplying a dozen at a time.

Out from the deck, he watched the goings. An intertwining of haphazard streets, nothing like the Utopia of his dreams. His lips curled in disdain, and his eyes wandered to the creatures huddling and tumbling at the corner street: those long-eared stupid ψs, another of his failed creation. So many bad decisions he wanted to undo, but he kept pushing them for later. A strong will was all that he needed: a strong will and a stronger muscular body.

He was now entering a steel chamber, Area 51, barricaded through and through. This was the pleasant part — his high chair with built-in intelligence switched temperature and softness to suit him. So much better. He heaved. After moments of sitting atop it, and he felt in control, a sense of being in command swept him, albeit briefly. Maybe the experiment to seed reason into an un-emotive chair wasn't that grave. It seemed to be working. With his thoughts steady, he was ready to focus on the trouble, so he peered at the screen.

There. The latest one was scampering on the streets. No logic whatsoever behind his movements — the vermin was beyond control limits. A few others tottered behind him, just as aimless. They bumped into streets, barricades, and shoots and seemed all too gung-ho about it. The virus was spreading fast. Though G-3 had sanitized it a dozen times,they had hit back stronger every time. There was no sense in curbing this foliage. They needed to do something different this time: extirpate it from its source and roots. But where was the source?

He traced back to the history of the rebel and dug down the data fed into his system. Nothing unusual. An ordinary sample from the last batch of humans. The task was excruciatingly unpleasant for his logic. Reluctant, he went ahead for a closer look anyway.

Now he was standing alongside the guy on that 3D screen. Mask-free, the man's face was an exhibit of shifting lewd expressions. Shoddy obscene hair matted with sweat clung to his head and chin, and his bared skin was marked with patches of soot. He strolled haphazardly, crossing signs, signals, marks, and lanes, tripping off them at places.

G-3 was irked beyond belief because of the scene unfolding in front of him. His lips crushed each other in disgust, and he couldn't look any longer. He had to go forward in time to see what this rag was up to. And just as he had predicted, he saw the man brazenly stretched out on the watch tower, his suit tossed aside and him naked in every way, his smile the most outrageous of all. Tufts of hideous hair protruded out from inappropriate places. His limbs extended out as if to overgrow themselves. G-3's blood boiled at sight. He stood on his toes out of anger. Outrageous. He clasped at the handles of his chair and snorted.

At the same time, he couldn't help noticing the beefy framework of the man:his thick muscular body strong and sprawled, taking more space than the G-3 ever could. He huffed.

That sound woke the rebel up, and he looked up. A smirk grew on his lips. As if he could see the G-3 through and through. His eyes were intense, his stance strong. The burning slash of pure will. G-3 retracted. He leaned back on his chair and stared at the screen for a long time. "He lost his fear. What's a human without fear?" He mumbled.

Contrary to himself, he felt awe growing in him. A tiny, powerless creature but something in him so overpowering, so undefeatable. As if he had crossed the realm beyond loss. In that instant, G-3 wanted what that man had. That unflinching will, an admire-worthy body. And he made the most unprecedented decision. To create the next G, a stronger version of himself, merging that man's will with his robot interminability. In a jiffy, he passed orders for the rag to be picked up alive. Though he questioned his decision bitterly once he regained his composure after getting up from the chair. But what was done was done. He had the reputation of inalterable orders.

He also ordered a new sanitation drive and introduced new rules. Full body suits with holes for eyes, ears, and heads in place of masks. That attire were doused in an overwhelming dull and repugnant fragrance.

But the source of the virus was still foggy. He pondered upon it and framed his questions differently. Could the virus have traveled from Earth? Did they bring it with them? Was it the same virus they quelled last time? Didn't look like it. His eyes skimmed through the long list of viruses and rebels quarantined for over 60 years. The numbers were steadily growing, however slow. He stared at the screen for longer than he usually did. His eyes were cold, his heart bitter as ice.

The list was still slipping through the screen.

G-3 walked out of his room into the shadowed balcony— an adjunct jutting out from his bunker perched on a Supertree. The spread was small but all that he needed. He could control the sun, rain, and wind with ceiling controls. Though he rarely paid an ounce of attention to it.

He walked in and stripped off his suit, layer by layer. First, the headgear, the gloves, arms, and leg cover, and finally, the bodice. The stench of his sweat was unbearable to his human nose. "Disperse," he commanded.

He stretched out on his bed. Nutrition pills piled on his side in tall stacks. He shut off his robot systems and scanned the chamber. Flat metal walls bending at perfect 90 degrees, installed to curb any curiosity, any aberration right at the roots— a template for perfection. At least this part was as he had wanted it to be.

His satisfaction was short-lived. It grew wings and flew out of the window the moment he saw something flicker in the silver ceiling. His eyes shrewdly searched the source of it, a ray of the grey sky had sneaked from the breaks in blinds and was now brazenly glistening on the silver ceiling. He'd never noticed those panes. Furious, he leapt to the rift, his heart unsteady as he inched closer. Those panes shrunk, exposing the grandiose view of mushrooming bunkers around, down below, far, and above.

They were everywhere, perched like thousand little birds on giant steel trees. And between them, tiny fly scoots flew carrying humanoids and humans in their body suits, creating slight buzzing sounds. It wasn't that they hadn't made any progress. He saw the robots that transformed at his wish. Theirs, and of others of their kind, status in the state was yet to be confirmed. Predictable and precise, they followed the instructions to the very end.

A ray of hope filled his heart: "Someday, they'll be autonomous, able to command, and the menace of sanitation drive will be done with." He shifted the panes. Greenery: trees, shrubs, climbers, flowers, and fruits. Nothing to see here. He moved it again to the ground level: humans walking in their lanes. His thought reading ESP device was flat. They weren't thinking; easier to track with full suits. The suits seemed to be working.

That order put his human brain at ease. He retreated to his bed and drifted to sweet sleep. But was brought back to his senses by the maniac beeping of his thought-reading device that jolted him awake. He pounced over to the shifting red dot on his screen. A boy. His thought "wha" flashing in big and bright words. G-3 reversed the tape. That blue suit was walking fine until something bright floated over him and seeded the thought "wha." G-3 froze the screen and magnified the speck. One of those things they kept in observatories: a butterfly?

The source of the virus. He issued a flurry of commands to quarantine all butterflies that might have escaped the observatories. A duo was discovered and quashed.

The rebel was now shackled and sprawled next to the G-3. A first of its kind, the operation had to extract the compulsive parts of his human brain and connect them with the unenterprising human nerves in G-3's head, along with it was tranformmed the human DNA that was to rebuild G-3's form, albeit slowly. The chair was quietly parked in the corner.

When Moon walked out of the containment, the humanoids barely noticed his changed form. Their secret was unlikely to come out because both Moon and the chair knew to keep their mouths shut.

Chapter 11: G1 and the Little Pinky Dump

Wu-C2 traveled further back in time. To a time when the Earth was still alive, still gasping for its last breaths.

Her first encounter with full humans wasn't very encouraging. She was parked in a deep well surrounded by famished versions of humans Moon talked about; dark wrinkled skin and bright yellow bulging eyes set on sunken cheeks; a muscle-less frame of nerves and bones. They sat bunched together and eerily still. She was one among them now: emaciated and wretched. A teenage black boy. A familiar feeling crept up her skin.

Their curled and matted hair set like a cap atop their bulbous heads. Tied to their ankles were broad blinking red bands. Hers was free. She scanned her surroundings and looked up at a tiny streak of light shining over her head. An escape? Could she climb up? She slid her arm to touch the facade behind her. It was good to grab.

The ground shook, and debris rained from the top. Flashes of intense light struck and set the space alight. She took a considerable amount of time to regain her sight.

Her eyes halted on the steep upward bend right above her, rendering of the hole in a bottle shape. Falling from that height could have meant suicide. Water oozed from cracks where the earth bled its soil like black blood. Running through fissures, it made mysterious steady ticks, one after another, counting its way to eternity. When Wu-C2 leaned, the drops made their way to her back and traced a chilling track from her neck to spine, ending up in a little pool where she sat. Bare broken roots of high trees punctured the ground sporadically, lending a perch to giant worms that dangled leisurely above. Wu-C2 felt her arm stiffen. The air was getting cooler, thicker, and infused with pungent smells.

Soon the cloak of darkness embraced all it touched. Wu-C2's teeth were chattering now, her breath coming in short gusts. The night was taking a harsher tone, and her limbs became frigid. One beefy creepy-crawly loosened its grip and plopped in front of her. Her eyes drifted dreamily to it. A desire grew in her heart to catch it, hold it and enclose it somewhere warm and safe.

The wiggly-wobbly squirmed and made desperate attempts to slither as far away as it could from Wu-C2. The light from glow worms receded, and those manlike bodies stole apprehensive glances.

"I wouldn't do that." A dry and flat voice floated to her. She turned to locate its source, the skimpily dressed slender man sitting right next to her. Everything about him was sharp as a razor. His piercing eyes, hawklike nose, and a pointed chin. And though his body was frail, the fineness of his features gave him an edge. Something about him exuded power and fear. And because Wu-C2 hadn't met G-1, she couldn't recognize him here — her first encounter with the first Universe General.

"I wouldn't do that if I were you." He repeated in a flat and cold voice.

The slithering thing escaped in a black hole, and the hole sealed its mouth swiftly. The place became hostile, cold, and still as ice. The steady rhythm of dripping water punctuated its quiet.

Once again, Wu-C2 was under the spotlight of big eyes,

crouched figures, and blank stares. Maybe this was the end of the world. But it looked too unhappening to be an end. Wu-C2 expected it to be big. Another Big Bang? Earth was supposed to be a happening place after all.

"Not really," the man said.

Wu-C2 readjusted her aching human butt. Could these people read their thoughts?

"Well, not all of them. Just me," he said casually. "But of course, you know it. Why are you even, well thinking?"

Wu-C2 fidgeted. Something inside her made her apprehensive of this formidable man, and she wanted to move away from him just as the worm did in their earlier encounter.

The almond-eyed man was watching her watching them. She twitched, sighed, rolled her eyes, and cracked her knuckles until she spotted an ant or two, and then her eyes hungrily chased them to the far end, merging into the muddy background.

Soon, they have all hauled up one person in a steel box at a time. Now that Wu-C2 was shaping into younger Haruto Amuro, she was regaining her memories, and the same feeling of anxiety came crawling up with it.

Haruto's head was aching. Smoke, fire, drizzle, and destruction were everywhere. The Earth he saw was a vortex of extreme bombings and chemical warfare, and the chances of its resurrection were nil because cockroaches had fled. Those critters fed on decaying matter and released trapped nitrogen into the soil, which plants used. Without them, Earth lost its ability to regenerate forests and other lives.

Dirt and diseases proliferated and accelerated the

exodus of other creatures. Most were burned, choked, and suffocated in the process.

The last few hundred humans dug deep holes in the Earth and cowered in them to save themselves from fire and acid rain.

The ground was coming apart. Mammoth-sized holes punctured Earth's surface, way up to its core. They bellowed and coughed up lava and toxins. Far away in the distance, mushroom-shaped cloud bulbs rose. These were the self-detonating H-bombs left by the humans that the cockroaches rigged on purpose before leaving the Earth. The sky was a darkened mass of smoke and grime, and the ground shook frequently. Ball-sized droplets of acid rain fell from the sky and left pink, freshly burnt spots on the skins they touched.

They called the G-1 Grecko. "Hello, Grecko. Good to see you back up." "Hello, Grecko, I heard they sent you down again." Up here, his eyes carried a different sheen. His voice was dry and exhausted, his skin chaffed and weathered.

Grecko closed his hands over his mouth and sent a hoot. A stubby little bird dashed down from the blackened skies. It perched on Grecko's shoulder and tittered. Grecko nodded. "I see. I see." The creases on his forehead deepened. "If only we could revive the real cockroaches."

He looked sternly at Haruto, and he felt his spine stiffen. "Listen, you. We can keep pretending that we don't know who you are and you don't know who we are, but we've got no time", he said. The pool in his eyes settled, and a new gleam emerged in them: one of hope and desperation. "I come straight to the point. Have you got the roach?" Haruto couldn't help noticing how those eyes shifted from warm almonds to cold speculative splits in a fleeting second.

He felt the wriggling pouch in his pocket.

A pandemonium rose on the sidelines and they turned to see its source. Two men dragged a human frame by its collar to the nearest crater. The creature hollered and was stomped in return.

"What's the count?" Grecko hollered to them.

"208. 1568 to go."

He nodded thoughtfully. "I see."

They released the man into an abutting hole, and his voice faded into the unknown darkness. The two men leaned to confirm his descent and turned to clap their hands to shred dust off them.

"Little pinky dump has quite an appetite," Grecko said and winked. When Haruto kept looking at him with his jaw hung way too loose, he said, "That was a cyborg, not of any consequence whatsoever."

A buzz grew on the horizon. The bunch freaked out.

"Roaches, they are coming."

They skittered to the nearest underground hole. Haruto followed, and Grecko took his sweet time lumbering after them.

"Come quick, Grecko, don't let the roaches see you." The frontman cried.

They were now all cramped up in a tiny hole. So close that their breath brushed one another's face. Their bodies pressed against each other from all sides. Some instinct made Haruto lay his hand on the bug inside his pocket. The sound of gliders grew in the sky. The men panted and whimpered louder, "The cockroaches have seen us. They are coming." Sobs, shiver and gasps took over the hole.

Dust rose high up as the gliders descended close to the ground. Haruto's ears went numb with the buzz.

Soon the roaches were standing in front of them. Huge ones with dagger-like sharp wriggling limbs that flipped the dirt high up in the air, creating a haze around.

The roaches headed straight for the men's hive. G-1's men skittered after one another, scrambling for the farthest spot. They moaned and whimpered and scuttled after one another. They screamed as the limbs of the roaches crawled up their skins, and their musty smell choked their noses. Grecko crouched. Haruto copied him.

The frightening buzz of the roaches got louder and more menacing. From the shifting vision pockets between trampled-over and decapitated men and gushing pools of blood, Haruto watched the cockroaches shred the standing men in pieces in single strikes. The men fell off in clumps as if massive bombs had detonated them.

Haruto gripped the wiggly sack in his pocket. Something stepped on his head, and he fell unconscious.

He woke up in a pool of blood with G-1 standing tall and staring at him with a smirk and bewildered look: "You survived."

The cockroaches had gone leaving a scattered mush of unrecognizable human organs and a lake of blood.

G-1's eyes veered to Haruto's bloody hand buried in his pocket. The sparkle in G-1's eyes returned. "You are one tough nut. Aren't you?"

Digging his fingers deep in the dirt, Haruto tried to crawl away from G-1. The creases on G-1's head deepened. "You cannot undo the history, Haruto, or should I say Moon or Wu-C2."

He crushed Haruto's bleeding leg under his boots. "I knew you'd be back to change the course. There's something about you that doesn't give up." Haruto heard a crack, followed by stabbing pain, possibly from his broken shin.

"But as you can see, the humans are gone, and I'm lined up to be the General, the ruler of the new world. You cannot possibly change that. Can you?"

Haruto closed his eyes, and with that came a memory of his younger years. A headline in the newspaper. "Man merges algorithms to create the biggest Deep Learning mechanism of all times: Saros."

"Enough of this. You've got to give that roach to me, Haruto. Come quick." G-1 extended his hand to Haruto, who could now taste the blood in his mouth and feel it drip on his ears.

Grecko's words were followed by uncomfortable silence.

Out on the horizon, another mushroom-shaped bomb exploded. This time way closer and bigger in size. A massive earthquake followed a wash of a blinding light. Grecko's breath was becoming uneven now. He grabbed Haruto by his leg and dragged him near the Little Pinky dump.

"This is your chance. Give it to me, now."

Haruto's torso was dangling over the Pinky Dump. G-1 reached out for his pocket. However, he couldn't grasp the wiggly pouch with Haruto's hand already buried there. Frustrated, he stood back and yanked Haruto's hands out. This time it fell out with the pouch still in its grip.

G-1's eyes grew to two greedy pools as he dived to snatch the squirmy little thing out of Haruto's grip.

Collecting the remaining few shreds of strength he got, Haruto thrust his body ahead. Seconds later, he descended into the Pinky Dump with the pouch still flapping in his hands.

Chapter 12: The Struggle for Survival

2222 on Earth.

G-4's bugs had tilled the grounds to great depths. As for cockroaches, Dodo's investigation was inconclusive. They released it into space and traced its connecting frequencies back to Earth. Now they were on with their search in the marshes. Their pursuit was so extensive that they had altered the planet's topography. The glaciers were shredded into little pieces, piling willy-nilly, and a new Everest stood on plain lands. Sea water seeped into the new lower lands and flooded them with toxic trash and formidable creatures.

G-4's introduction to the silent life breeding in deep waters came as an abrupt revelation. One of his bugs hovered over a curling crocodile-shaped creature. The creature jumped high up in the air with heavy-duty fins-like wings and swallowed it whole. G-4 heard a heavy splash and a crunch of his munched bug as the massive creature dived back into the water.

A symphony of similar splashes peaked. G-4's bugs crashed and dropped like flies. The creatures crushed them comfortably in batches with shredder-like jaws and high-acid stomach fluids.

The last time G-4 heard about Earth's crocodiles, they went extinct under contaminated waters. This new development flummoxed him. He didn't know that it was just a trailer for the destruction that was about to come. Giant tentacles uncoiled underwater, and a pair of slit eyes pasted on a pockmarked round head crept out every now and then from the black muck. As slyly as they appeared, they disappeared in the water, swiftly swooping buckets of the bugs trapped in their warts.

If there was one lesson that the roaches took from their Pleritus mishap, it was to keep their distance from murky waters. They took to dry lands, even the ones surrounding volcanos. Sitting inside their titanium bores, they drilled deep down into the earth's crust sucking and spitting the mud, sands, muck, and fossils. Dodo's trails had led them to this point.

The seawater around Moon's chamber was receding fast, rushing to the lower lands, further placating the already quietened volcano, diffusing its wrath. At best, it was retching dwarf outflows sporadically. The awful creatures camouflaged underwater depths were now emerging in bundles. Their strangeness intrigued Moon. Outwardly distinct, they all carried the same deadly, sharp, poisonous undercurrent.

The unusual commotion at Earth attracted Saros' attention. With its center of gravity shaken, the planet was now tilting the other way. This new development in a passive planet was new. Saros directed its algorithms to drill down to the roots of it. There was another reason for this interest too. Following the whale debacle, Saros had received a complaint from the Pleritus crabs, who had filed a case of interruption and productivity loss against Vespa. Their despair was compounded by the disappearance of the wish monkey and Wu-C2.

The news traveled to Vespa, that got busy belligerently tracking askew frequencies emerging from Earth.

Sitting on his chair, with gray tufts of wispy hair sprouting at various places in his body and a hunched back,

Moon mulled over his options. There were only two. One: Throw himself and his chamber to ants and remove the traces of Woozy Do forever. Two: Submit to Saros.

The earth above him rattled. Something was inching closer, and Moon scanned his screens. The bugs in his chamber began scuttling amok. Had someone located him? Moon checked on the G-4 and cockroaches again. They were still screwing up the distant lands. Right above him, on the land, was a sprawled sea pig with no face as such but a puncture in its face with a long slimy tongue that stretched out like a tail out of its mouth. Moon's best estimate was that the creature was thrown out of the water and was scrambling for life. He thanked the layers of earth between his chamber and the big blob on the surface.

"Whoa. That's next-level creepiness."

"Welcome back, Dracko," Moon said without turning to see him.

Dracko's update on Utopia wasn't very encouraging: "Well, not something that you'd look forward to. Cyborgs are almost gone. Some terminated, and others systems failed. And with them gone, humanoids and robots don't have much to do."

"So, this indeed is the end. I'm beginning to wonder if what we did was right."

Dracko raised his brows, and they almost touched his forehead. "Well, that's unlike Moon. Your human heart is sure at work."

"Look at this mess. Utopia demolished. Woozy Do lost. Witches on the radar. Earth more wretched. Who has gained anything out of it?"

Silence ensued as they watched the G-4's bugs struggling with various nasty-looking water creatures anchored to the shores in hundreds. G-4's bugs subjugated even before they came close to any damage. They huddled and crashed.

Dracko roared, "Well, that's a sight to behold. Something I haven't seen for long."

He looked at the creatures in the chamber scuttling and huddling in the farthest corner.

"You aren't the nastiest looking things after all." He said and reminisced: "Talking about nasty creatures, I've got some reassuring news. Saros is investigating the roaches against the Pleritus crabs' complaints of interference. It has opened communication lines for planets, and Vespa is no longer the controlling commission."

They sat for long under a spell of crushing silence.

"Any signal from her?"

"No. It's way too risky now."

"You'll lose her for sure this way. We've got to call her back. She is our only hope after cyborgs." He was pained to speak the improbable. "Just this time. I swore to keep my distance from those damn witches, but we don't have much choice."

Moon thought and nodded. This surprising squall of generosity from Dracko was amusing to him.

Dracko was gone, and with him, the chair disappeared too.

In Bella- Dilla, the Pink lady wasn't too pleased to see this uninvited visitor and looked suspiciously at her mongoose, who promptly looked away.

"My lady, we share our displeasure," Dracko said. "You

don't want me here, and I don't want myself here too. But we've got a task at hand."

She crossed her arms and said: "Bella-Dilla has nothing to do with the sterile tasks of those hateful planets. We've already lost enough."

Dracko passed a glance at the mongoose. "Well, in that case, you must know that the secret existence of your sphere is no more overlooked by the Vespa cockroaches who are now hunting every single node of the universe for aberrations. And you've got quite a handful of them here."

The Pink lady sidled with her mongoose for an urgent consultation.

Hungry Bizzy was quietly pleased with being alone with a stranger. She took the opportunity of the brief distraction and began her humming…. "Woo wa ri rum."

A couple of wild voices joined her croon.

Dracko rolled his eyes up. "Oh, come on. I am a hologram. Can't you see? No love juice here. Shoo. Keep your distance, you nasty witch."

Bizzy retreated and hissed: "Maybe we've got to broaden our menu."

The Pink lady flew back promptly. "We have a word." She said.

"And that is."

"Bella-Dilla doesn't meddle with the pursuits of the mortals, and we would like to keep it that way."

"Very well. In that case, my lady, I must tell you that your secret is out with the human who was here. The roaches are looking for her; if they catch her, your secret will be out with them in no time. It's beyond me to fathom what they'll do after knowing that Bella-Dilla foiled one of their biggest plans."

A dark cloud grew over her as she glared at her mongoose.

Dracko resisted the urge to smirk and spoke to hungry Bizzy. "Also, I must tell you, with all the humans gone, you won't get any love juice either."

That was enough to miff Bizzy, who resumed her whimpering. "A world without love juice ain't a bright world at all. Pink lady or not."

Other witches, too, looked displeased about Dracko's suggestion.

"Oh, shut up. I'll deal with you once this is over." The Queen glared at Bizzy, the dark storm over her head growing.

She now looked reproachfully at Dracko. "Hologram. You talk too much, and your big mouth will get you in trouble soon."

Dracko nodded.

She frowned at him and sighed: "Just this one time. We get the human back, and you vow to keep our secret."

Soon a range of frequencies flew out from Bella-Dilla, and Wu-C2 was pulled back from Soak. Her Soul Machine came hurtling after.

It can't be said that she was happy at this unwelcome sight. With both witches and Dracko, it was compound contempt.

Bizzy drooled, and saliva ran from the corners of her lips. Witches looked at Wu-C2 with expectant eyes.

"The human has our secret. The secret dies with it."

Thw witches cornered Wu-C2.

Dracko had no time to think. In his haste, he commanded the Soul Machine to take Wu-C2 to the first place he had in his mind. To Moon's Earth.

Considering the circumstances, this was the worst he could have done.

Soon as the Soul Machine veered out of Bella-Dilla, both G-4 and the cockroaches realigned their trajectory to this strange contraption's landing, i.e., Moon's mound. Saros, too detected the aberration and channeled its troops to the target.

A sharp jolt from the G-4's herculean arm sent the machine tumbling into the marshes. His bugs jumped to their job and restrained it in place, cutting its sensors to keep their discovery from cockroaches.

But roaches already hovered over the scene darkening the sky and blocking the sun rendering a bright summer day into a starless pitch-black night. Their deafening buzz made Wu-C2 crouch in the corner of the machine.

Contrarily, the roach inside the machine retrieved its strength and latched itself to the front screen, flipping its wings rapidly to attract the attention of its kin cockroaches outside. The roaches on the outside caught its cry and collided with G-4's bugs tossing them away from the machine.

Sparks flew out from G-4's frame. He he took giant leaps and pounced at the machine to look inside. With one swift shove of his arm, he dislodged the roaches clinging to the screen and looked straight at Wu-C2. "Moon's girl," his voice boomed. He joined his arms and smashed the screen. A void grew, and the roach inside the machine flew out from the crevice. G-4 gave a sharper blow, and the screen was shattered open.

The buzz and the booms were deafening for Wu-C2, who could not make sense of the rapid happenings. G-4 towered over the machine and reached his arm inside to grab Wu-C2. It constricted around Wu-C2's forearm and yanked her out of the Soul machine with a sharp jolt.

With Wu-C2 dangling out in the open, the riot riveted on her. The cockroaches swarmed around G-4 as he stomped, springing Wu-C2 in his arm and thrusting the cockroaches away with the rest of his limbs.

In this frenzy, both the cockroaches and G-4 overlooked the ground that was getting flooded with the creatures of the water. They slithered and scuttled surreptitiously over the high and low grounds. The giant octopus sneaked out from the waters and observed the cacophony from the sidelines. With his stomach satiated with G-4's bugs and a cat's curiosity in his head, it was now looking for adventure and not just food. His eyes veered to the towering G-4, walking with shuddering steps dangling Wu-C2 in one arm, attracting too much attention.

It snakingly slithered its tentacles to reach G-4's feet. Still a few feet away from its grasp, the G-4 tightened his grasp around WU-C2's arm, opening a deep red gash in it. Blood lined their path. Roaches hovered over and latched themselves to G-4, blanketing his view making him stumble a few steps over the dead sea pig. He slipped over the rotting flesh landing under the reach of the giant cephalopod.

The creature was quick to act. Its tentacle ringed around G-4's feet and shrunk, strengthening its hold on G-4. And before G-4 knew it, he was getting shoved and drowned in deep waters.

    Wu-C2

Under muddy water, a panorama of many thousand formidable creatures surrounded them: faceless sea pigs, vampire squids with swordlike tentacles, alien-faced gulper eels, giant black man o wars floating at leisure, multiple-headed poisonous sea snakes. All curious to make acquaintance with the new entrants. The cephalopod shoved Wu-C2 and G-4 to deeper depths, into pitch black waters.

A hybrid of shark, swordfish, and Metapseudes closed in and poked Wu-C2 with its big snout. The jets of water oozing out from its nostrils hit Wu-C2's eyes and blood from her open wound seeped into its mouth. The creature was revolted. Years of munching over metal had it uninterested in the human flesh. It quickly floated up and snapped on the G-4's metal arm that was constricting Wu-C2. Crushed in between its shredder-like jaws, tG-4's limb cracked and split. Other creatures darted to G-4, deflecting Wu-C2, who was now floating up courtesy of the air pockets trapped in G-4's clipped arm. The last time Wu-C2 saw G-4, he was sinking into the deepening darkness with his cold eyes still pinned on her.

Wu-C2 found herself splayed in a pool of blood upon the marshes. And a swarm of cockroaches hovered over her.

Chapter 13: The Verdict

Dracko realized his blunder soon as it was administered. After veering Wu-C2 back to the heart of extinction, he had no option but to look for immediate help. He left the crooning witches to themselves.

Like always, his first refuge was his favorite feisty Lucas' Rhinos.

He hovered over the Lucas skies seeking a sign of them. The sight of famished animals depressed him, but he kept the thought of waking them off to some other dreadful day.

"Whoa, you are all juiced-up," was all he said.

Luck was on his side. A dust storm grew on the horizon, and Rhinos appeared, trampling, toppling and waking the stunned animals on their way.

Convincing the Rhinos was a cinch. All he needed to say was: "I've got an adventure for you, a fight and it involves the roaches."

They pounced upon this once-in-a-lifetime opportunity and huffed, puffed, and stomped their feet even before Dracko finished his talk. Staunch patrons of quick action, Rhinos were never enthusiastic about any details.

But there was one trouble. The Soul machine, courtesy of its last encounter with the Rhinos, wasn't very encouraged. It stood uncooperative, still as ice. Dracko wheedled and needled it to pull the Rhinos to Earth. Two promises were made: the creatures would resist their urge to kick it upon all costs or risk getting dropped in space, and having done its best , the Soul Machine would retire back to Pleritus after its last task. For the sake of the promised fun that was to follow at the end of the ride, the Rhinos agreed. And so, they were on their journey, donning their glasses and oxygen masks.

Getting the trees to the task was tricky. More than anything, Dracko was incensed by their slow drawl.

"My majesties, Utopia and Earth need your help. The last human you prided is in grave danger of extinction from the roaches of Vespa. You are no stranger to their insidious deeds."

He waited a lot of time before they rustled in response to his request:

"We don't meddle.."

"For centuries, you've been estranged by Saros and roaches equally. It's a shame that the Universe seeks its pilotage from an unfeeling bunch of algorithms that can sift data but cannot add any fresh insight on its own. The world will be better run by the knowledge and wisdom of the trees."

The trees swayed to his proposition. It was fetching. But they took their own sweet time to rustle their response.

"Humans deserve no mercy. And we bow to none. But trees have always done their duty. They have always provided shelter to seekers. And so will we this time. Whoever needs the truth must come to us. To Pleritus. The trees are ready to bear witness to the ills of the cockroaches and acquaint Saros with the truth."

What Moon saw back on Earth was no less than a nightmare, a war of the worst: cockroaches and water creatures wrestling in the muck, slashing butchering one another. Entangling and toppling , amassing in messy bunches. On far and few instances when the cockroaches won, they shredded the creatures apart in unrecognizable mush.

But for the most part, the water creatures prevailed. Kindled by the taste of the G-4 and his bugs, they were now out scampering for more meals, and the metal cockroaches were topping their list.

With much difficulty, Dracko spotted Wu-C2, who lay gasping for breath under the swarm of cockroaches. Deducing Wu-C2 as a bait, a wide-jawed crocodile had perched atop her. The roaches darted to her in droves, and water creatures huddled to snap at them. A massive heap of wrigglers encircled her.

Wu-C2 heard a familiar thud. The Rhinos were coming, squelching, stomping, and kicking the cockroaches a hundred times. Her fears compounded with getting crushed under Rhinos as the latest entry. She grappled to get up from under the crocodile. Taking hold of the uneven terrain around her with her fingers digging deep, she exerted to crawl out. The crocodile sensed her escape and pressed her even more.

Dracko saw her extending hand and hovered over the heap. "Yo roaches, what do you think you are up to now? Maggots getting munched over by the gator. Yeah, that's the way to do it. Dart straight into its mouth. Spot on. GetShredded to pieces. That's majestic. Who needs enemies when you are stupid yourself?"

He began his high-pitched song, and his voice rose steadily, tumbling, dislodging, and slipping cockroaches. Just when things couldn't have gone more chaotic, the volcano erupted, gushing tons of lava and smoke out and pushing the temperature many degrees up.

In the far and few instances when Moon's seat wasn't shaking or throbbing, he tried to focus on Woozy. The scene was a gridlock, with no party nearing any conclusion. The roaches were infinite, and so seemed the water creatures' appetite. There was no way Wu-C2 could have escaped the hold of that crocodile.

But then something unprecedented happened. The cockroaches in the sky skittered to show the blue clouds, and a massive disc hovered above. A thing of fables:the first occasion, Saros had ventured out in the open to take stock of the situation. Corporate crabs had worked their magic.

A massive cavity at the bottom of the disc opened up, and Wu-C2 was sucked in along with some prominent cockroaches.

Later..

They stood in front of a humongous glass wall. Monumental in scale and embellished extensively across ends, the wall ran records of Moon, Wu-C2, G-4, and the cockroaches. Wu-C2 saw herself crushing the roach. An eerie silence pervaded. The ways of Saros were simple. If you were innocent, you were set free; if you were guilty, they wiped you and your records out forever. No one knew that you ever existed. Of course, you weren't expected to present your defense, for they had all their records. And records they referred for everything.

On the side screen, the trees continued with their testimony.

"The roaches, they killed humans. Not that the humans were worthy of getting saved. But the roaches bullied the world."

Moon was summoned too. From the last time Wu-C2 saw him, he looked old and fragile, with folds in his face and a hunch on his back. He passed a feeble smile at Woozy Do and winked. Wu-C2 smiled in return.

The vetting began. A voice boomed, summoning Wu-C2. "Travel in time is a crime. Saros has always emphasized the importance of maintaining the natural order of things. We had our difficult lessons from humans meddling with it. We democratized the planets and gave them equal powers. And we celebrated a peaceful Universe for many centuries.

But you, Wu-C2, have been replaying the blunders of humans, your kind. You allowed your curiosity to overpower you. And see where it has led us again.

Silence.

That's one truth. But there's another that you are the last full human we have, and with that roach, you've brought hopes of repopulating the Earth again. Your intentions were just. As much as we want to curb human greed and lust for power, we resent seeing them in oblivion. For the sake of a better world, you'll be set free on Earth once we wipe out the traces of time travel from your memory."

Moon tried to suppress his glee and wished for the presence of his friend, Dracko. The occasion called for a celebration. But his pleasure was short-lived. Soon Saros announced his name. "Moon. The linchpin of this treacherous voyage. It's a shame that you've endangered your own cyborg's and other planets' safety. Most of all, you damaged the peace of Utopia, the one state you had sworn to protect. As a representative of the State, this is an unpardonable crime. From the records that we have here of your perpetual deviations, you don't seem to improve:

time travel, lethal experiments, secret chambers, and what not. Haruto's spirit in you seems to derive pleasure from rebellion. And that's an incorrigible trait. Leaving you to your own devices can prove precarious. Saros presents you with two choices: Become a full human and perish in a few years on Earth or surrender your memory and status as G-3 and survive as a common cyborg."

Though the message was stern, Moon still struggled to contain his smile and nodded cordially.

Saros didn't go that easy on the cockroaches. "Saros is concerned with the crimes of cockroaches. Peace and freedom are at the very foundation of the New Universe. Any entity meddling with the order of the universe, and that too in a treacherous way, threatens the whole of it. Power is severe in the hands of the self-absorbed.

Contrary to common belief, the lust for control and power clearly indicates inferiority. And it seems despite many centuries of peaceful co-existence, the cockroaches have failed to reconcile with their image of themselves. Cockroaches must know that their true worth is reflected inside out. The Universe merely reflects your opinion of it. And because the cockroaches have been harboring a skewed perception, they'd been acting treacherously.

In the past, the cockroaches have been condoned for the extirpation of humans as a simple act of piled-up revenge, but their hankering for power is now threatening the entire universe, and it cannot go unchecked. They are summoned to relinquish their robotic form, resume their natural state and help Wu-C2 repopulate Earth. And before all that, they need to clear Earth of all debris they discarded. Saros believes that hard work is the only way to hone self-esteem."

In a follow-up order, Saros directed the stunned creatures of Lucas to be carried over back to Earth, where they could wake up and live a regular life.

The party that was dismayed by the sentence was the Rhinos. With the roaches gone and no creatures left to awaken, there wasn't much to kick around. But their disappointment was short-lived. They were tasked with keeping the water creatures civil and zone bound. A seemingly more significant challenge, this considerably warmed them up.

Chapter 14: The Beginning

Wu-C2 found herself desperately scratching her leg. She scooped out a handful of mud and rubbed it on her arms and back. Though with the amount of layers of mud on her, there was no scope left to put anymore over her skin anywhere.

She put one layer, scratched all over and then another and yet another. Out in the distance, a scabby dog with a dangling dead squirrel in his mouth watched her with amusement. Their eyes met. A gush of saliva flooded Wu-C2's mouth, and before she knew it, it drooped from her sunken lips. The dog looked sideways at Wu-C2 with wary eyes, and their eyes met briefly once again before he made a decision. With little pounces, he moved away, his tail between his legs. But Wu-C2 wasn't to miss it. Not this time. She leapt after the dog pouncing over the hurdles and tumbling, getting scratched from the spiky shrubs. The dog whined and scampered faster. Wu-C2 picked up. Her eyes hooked on the squirrel. Her panting mouth drooling even more. Her hungry stomach roaring at the anticipation of this juicy meal.

Once, she was so close that she almost grabbed him by his hind leg. But she had to stop to address an urgent itch, and he gained the distance swiftly. The sun was already up and burning. But none of them was anywhere near to giving up. Then they reached a dead-end. A towering fence of spiky dried-up poisonous plants stood in between both and the trashed forest. The dog was breathless, and so was Wu-C2. He made a futile attempt to turn around, but Wu-C2 charged and blocked his way. Their eyes pinned, their paws piercing the mud. The hound's mind was hurtling like a storm, a hard choice between Wu-C2 and the hurtsome barrier. He drew back, rallied all his strength, and pounced over the fence tearing his limbs at various places where they kissed the spikes.

Wu-C2 jumped after him. Halfway she fell flat on the bed of spikes and yelped. The dog, who now stood at a safe distance, licked its wound and watched Wu-C2 squirm from the corners of his eyes. Their eyes met again. Wu-C2 pushed her scabbed palms on the spiky bed and exerted to get up. If not for the tattered piece of cloth on her waist, she almost got up and ran again. But that piece was stiffer now with all the mud and dust trying to attach itself to various objects in the vicinity; she was yanked back, this time turning and falling flat on her face. Her teeth digging deep into her human lip, splitting it into two bulks. The dog was out of sight. Wu-C2 tore away the damn cloth with her teeth. She was naked now. Her sleek butts pressed against a heap of crushed bushes. The itching was back, and she scratched her head with the tip of her overgrown fingernails blackened by the gummy dirt.

Ahead of her lay a path with marked hoofs: a cow or a horse. She took the path, faltering on her four limbs. It was a long since the last time she stood on two, and she had almost forgotten about it. Along the path ran a river of black waters tarnished with traces of grease, oil, metal, and chemicals. She sprinted, affixing her eye on the tracks bumping into tree stumps, stones, shrubs, and trash, pacing before the animal got far.

Something brilliant shone and flipped in the river right ahead of her. A fish. Wu-C2 found herself drooling and hyperventilating again. She forgot the tracks and leapt for the shiny thing. But it was a junked tin sheet, a piece of trash like the rest. Wu-C2 peered over the stale water patch and saw her reflection on a floating metal sheet. An oval, egg-shaped face with a depressed, almost non-existent head, protruded cheeks, button nose, and big glassy almond eyes. She tapped on the tin sheet, and it sank. When the ripples settled, she wasn't the only one in the reflection. Behind her stood the imposing G-4. He grabbed her by her hair, whatever little was left of it, and dragged her back to the tracks she came from, Wu-C2's torso purging the trails left by the animal.

He pointed at the workers on the other side. Wu-C2 squirmed and walked to the group with odd steps resisting the urge to drop down on fours. Here were the dozen others like her: short, emaciated ones with oval depressed heads, button noses, flaky skin, and big eyes. Ahead of them lay a giant dead Vespa robot. At first, they tried to push it with bare hands and sticks. It didn't budge. Then they decided to dig the mud underneath it. So, they kept spades and other tools aside and started digging the mud with their bare hands.

Up above in the sky, a scooter flew. Two Σsrode in it.

"Error. Odd chances. You've been digging the wrong side."

Meanwhile, Wu-C2's team had dug the ground substantially from opposite sides. They pushed the boulder from both sides, negating the efforts from the other end. The ones on the higher side gained momentum and overpowered, pushing the robot through the cliff. It rolled, crushing the others in its way. Around sunset, Wu-C2 was lifted by the men in scooters. While Wu-C2 was raised high up in the sky, she saw heaps of trash on the horizon outlined by the same black river she saw. The earth looked like a bubbling stew with smoke rising from all directions.

She regained consciousness tied up on the sanitization counter. Her limbs stretched and fastened tight to a metal base. They'd scraped the mud off her skin. It was burning now and had baby pink under skin.

Moon stood in front of her, smiling in his complete human form. His cataract-laden eye reflected amusement. "Ho Ho Ho Woozy Do. It looks like you've made quite a big progress there."

Wu-C2 tried to smile, but it came out faint and awkward at best. "What happened?"

"You caught the virus from the water critters."

"I saw G-4."

Moon smiled. "In the world of that virus, everything is hostile."

"What happened to the roach?"

"Well, you'll see for yourself soon. To begin with, it is still alive."

An ache rose in Wu-C2's leg.

"You need to grow some skin Woozy Do before you flex your limbs."

"Flex. Input needed."

"Ho Ho Ho Woozy Do. No inputs for you anymore. The roaches had deactivated your robot side, and Saros wants to keep it this way. And they have deactivated most of my memory too. So, I guess you'll have to discover on your own."

Watching a flash of disappointment flush Wu-C2's face. He continued: "So here's the last input for you. However, you have already been acting on it. Follow your heart."

And indeed, when Wu-C2 looked back, she realized

she'd been doing precisely that "following her heart.".

Wu-C2 now heard a familiar sound, "Swish. Swish"

Dracko appeared. His frown was intact like always. "Oh. Well yes. It's Wu-C2 again. And let me see what you're up to. The hologram grew, and his eyes widened. "I see. A human. Are you a human now, Wu-C2? Hmm. Interesting."

Dracko had come to pick Moon. They had a lot of sightseeing before Dracko returned to Utopia, and Moon died a human death. Moon boarded the shoot, and before Wu-C2 could speak, he bid adieu: "I'll see you around, Woozy Do. Ho ho ho. Lots to see before I perish." He said and flew out. His chair was now parked by Wu-C2's side.

During the days that followed, Wu-C2 drifted between varying streams of consciousness.

When she woke up, her newly formed skin felt smooth like ice. She was hoisted up to an extraordinary view. Amidst the black debris, on an elevated platform of thousand pillars, stood a lush green island with a fresh fountain of its own. Following their massive reputation uphaul in front of Saros, the trees had agreed to do their bit to populate the Earth again. And skittering cockroaches were shy like they had been in their earlier days, doing their job of cleaning up secretly.

The critters from Moon's chamber were now free for the first time. As for the chair, it was Wu-C2's turn to sit on it. At first, she felt awkward, but an unusual calm followed a few moments of anxiousness. She heaved and said: "Well, now that we're here, let's see what can be done."

www.ingramcontent.com/pod-product-compliance
Lightning Source LLC
Chambersburg PA
CBHW030318160726
47992CB00005B/2066